Pippi Goes Aboard

Books by Astrid Lindgren
Pippi Longstocking
Pippi Goes Aboard
Pippi in the South Seas

Emil's Clever Pig
Emil and the Great Escape
Emil and the Sneaky Rat

Lotta Says 'No!'
Lotta Makes a Mess

Karlson Flies Again
Karlson on the Roof
The World's Best Karlson

The Brothers Lionheart

Ronia, the Robber's Daughter

Pippi Goes Aboard

Astrid Lindgren

Translated by Marianne Turner
Illustrated by Tony Ross

OXFORD
UNIVERSITY PRESS

OXFORD
UNIVERSITY PRESS

Great Clarendon Street, Oxford OX2 6DP

Oxford University Press is a department of the University of Oxford.
It furthers the University's objective of excellence in research, scholarship,
and education by publishing worldwide in

Oxford New York

Auckland Cape Town Dar es Salaam Hong Kong Karachi
Kuala Lumpur Madrid Melbourne Mexico City Nairobi
New Delhi Shanghai Taipei Toronto

With offices in

Argentina Austria Brazil Chile Czech Republic France Greece
Guatemala Hungary Italy Japan South Korea Poland Portugal
Singapore Switzerland Thailand Turkey Ukraine Vietnam

Oxford is a registered trade mark of Oxford University Press
in the UK and in certain other countries

First published as *Pippi Langstrump gar Ombord* by Rabén & Sjögren 1956
First published in this edition 2006

British Library Cataloguing in Publication Data available

All foreign and co-production rights shall be handled by Kerstin Kvint Agency AB,
Stockholm, Sweden

ISBN 978-0-19-275482-0

10 9 8

Printed in Great Britain

Paper used in the production of this book is a natural,
recyclable product made from wood grown in sustainable forests.
The manufacturing process conforms to the environmental
regulations of the country of origin.

Contents

1
Pippi still lives at Villekulla Cottage

If a stranger, coming to the little Swedish town, should one day happen to find himself in a particular place on the outskirts, he would see Villekulla Cottage. Not that the cottage is much to look at: it is rather a tumble-down old cottage with an overgrown garden round it, but the stranger might perhaps pause to wonder who lived there, and why there was a horse in the porch. If it was really late and almost dark, and if he caught sight of a little girl striding round the garden looking as if she had no intention of going to bed, he might think:

'I wonder why that little girl's mother doesn't see that she goes to bed? Other children are fast asleep by this time.'

If the little girl came up to the gate—and she would be certain to do so, because she enjoyed talking to people—then he would have the chance of taking a good look at her, and would probably think:

'She's one of the freckliest and most red-headed children I've ever seen.'

Afterwards perhaps he would think:

'Freckles and red hair are really rather nice—at least when a person has such a happy appearance as this child.'

It would perhaps interest him to know the name of this little red-head who was strolling about by herself in the dusk, and if he was close to the gate, he might ask:

'What's your name?'

A merry voice would reply:

'Pippilotta Provisiona Gaberdina Dandeliona Ephraims-daughter Longstocking, daughter of Captain Ephraim Longstocking, formerly the terror of the seas, now Cannibal King: but everybody calls me Pippi!'

When she said that her father was a Cannibal

King, she firmly believed it, because he had once been blown into the water and disappeared when Pippi and he had been out sailing on the sea. Since Pippi's father was somewhat stout, she was absolutely sure he had not been drowned. It seemed reasonable to suppose that he had been washed ashore on an island and become king over all the cannibals there, and this is exactly what Pippi thought had happened. If the traveller went on chatting to Pippi, he would find out that, except for a horse and a monkey called Mr Nelson, she lived quite alone at Villekulla Cottage. If he had a kind heart, he probably could not help thinking:

'How does the poor child live?'

He really need not have worried about that.

'I'm rich as a troll,' Pippi used to say. And she was. She had a whole suitcaseful of golden coins which her father had given her, and she managed splendidly without either mother or father. Since there was no one to tell her when to go to bed, Pippi told herself. Sometimes she did not tell herself until about ten o'clock, because Pippi had never believed that it was necessary for children to go to bed at seven. That was the time when you had the most fun. So the stranger should not be surprised at seeing Pippi striding round the garden, although the sun had set and the air was getting chilly, and Tommy and Annika had been tucked up in bed for ages. Tommy and Annika were Pippi's playmates, who lived in the house next to Villekulla Cottage. They had both a father and a mother, and both the father and the mother believed that it was best for children to go to bed at seven.

If the stranger lingered after Pippi had said goodnight and had left the gate, and if he saw Pippi go up to the porch and lift the horse high in her strong arms and carry him out into the garden, he would surely rub his eyes and wonder if he was dreaming.

'What a remarkable child this is,' he would say to himself. 'I do believe she can lift the horse! This is the most remarkable child I've ever seen!'

In that he would be right. Pippi was the most remarkable child—at least in that town. There may be more remarkable children in other places, but in that little town there was no one like Pippi Longstocking, and nowhere in the world, neither in that town nor anywhere else, was there anyone so strong as she was.

2
Pippi goes Shopping

It was a beautiful spring day, the sun was shining, the birds were twittering and snow water ran in all the ditches. Tommy and Annika came skipping over to Pippi's. Tommy had brought two lumps of sugar for the horse, and both he and Annika stopped for a moment in the porch to pat it before they went inside to see Pippi. Pippi was asleep when they came in. Her feet were on the pillow, and her head was far down under the bedclothes. She always slept that way. Annika pinched her big toe and called:

'Wake up!'

Mr Nelson, the little monkey, was already awake and sitting on the lamp hanging from the ceiling. Presently there was movement underneath the bedclothes, and suddenly a red head popped out. Pippi opened her bright eyes, grinned, and said:

'Oh, it's you! I dreamt it was my father, the Cannibal King, looking to see if I had any corns.'

She sat up, put her legs out and pulled on her stockings, one brown and the other black.

' 'Course not! You don't get any corns from these,' she said, putting on her big, black shoes which were exactly twice as long as her feet.

'Pippi,' said Tommy, 'what shall we do? Annika and I have a holiday today.'

'Ooh,' said Pippi, 'let's think up something nice. We can't dance round the Christmas tree, because we threw it out three months ago. Otherwise we could have played Christmas games all morning. It would be fun to dig for gold, but we can't do that either, because we don't know where the gold is. Besides, most of the gold is in Alaska, and you can't move an inch there for gold diggers. No, we must think of something else.'

'Yes,' said Annika, 'something *really* nice.'

Pippi did her hair into two tight plaits that stuck straight out. She was thinking.

'What about going into town to do some shopping?' she said at last.

'But we haven't got any money,' said Tommy.

'I have,' said Pippi, and to prove it she went at once and opened her suitcase which was full of gold coins. She took out a large handful and put the coins in a big pocket in the front of her apron.

'Now, if I could only find my hat,' she said, 'I'd be ready to start off.' The hat was nowhere to be seen. First Pippi took a look in the wood-box, but strange to say it was not there. Then she looked in the breadbin, but there was nothing in it except a suspender, a broken alarm clock, and a small rusk. Finally she looked on the hat rack, but found only a frying pan, a screw-driver, and a piece of cheese.

'There's no order in nothing, and I can't find everything,' said Pippi irritably. 'Though I've missed the cheese for a long time: good thing that was found.'

'Come here, hat,' she shouted, 'are you coming shopping or not? If you don't come at once, you'll be too late!'

No hat came.

'Well, it has no one but itself to blame when it's so obstinate, but I won't put up with any complaints when I come back,' she said sternly.

Soon afterwards they could be seen walking along the road leading to the centre of the town, Tommy and Annika and Pippi with Mr Nelson on her shoulder. The sun shone brilliantly, the sky was very blue, and the children were very happy. There was a gurgling in the ditch beside the road. It was a deep ditch with lots of water in it.

'I like ditches,' said Pippi, and without further ado she stepped down into the water. It went above her knees, and when she jumped really hard it splashed Tommy and Annika.

'I'm a boat,' she said, and ploughed through the water. As she said this she stumbled and went under.

'I mean a submarine,' she went on quite unperturbed as soon as her head was above water again.

'Oh, Pippi,' said Annika anxiously, 'you're wet through.'

'What's wrong with that?' said Pippi. 'Who said children must be dry? Cold showers are supposed to be good for you, I've heard. It's only in this country they've got the idea that children shouldn't walk in ditches. In America the ditches are so full of children that there isn't any room for the water. They stay in the ditches all the year round. In the winter, of course, the children freeze into them, and their heads pop out through the ice. Their mothers have to take fruit salad and steak and kidney pudding to them, because they can't go home for dinner. But, you bet, they're as strong and fit as can be.'

The little town looked lovely in the spring sunshine. The narrow, cobbled streets seemed to wind their way anyhow between the rows of houses. Nearly every house was surrounded by a small garden with snowdrops and crocuses in it. There were lots of shops in the little town. On this fine spring day plenty of people were going in and out of them, and the shop bells rang continuously. The housewives arrived with baskets on their arms to buy coffee and sugar and soap and butter.

Quite a lot of children were out buying toffees or packets of chewing gum, but most of them had no money to spend, and these poor things stood outside the shops and could only *look* at all the sweets behind the glass.

When the sun was shining most brightly, three small people appeared in the High Street. They were Tommy, Annika, and Pippi—a very moist Pippi, who left a wet trail behind her as she sauntered along.

'Aren't we lucky?' said Annika. 'Look at all the shops, and we have a pocketful of gold coins!'

Tommy was so happy when he thought of this that he jumped for joy.

'Shall we start then?' said Pippi. 'First of all I'd like to buy a piano.'

'But, Pippi,' said Tommy, 'you can't play the piano!'

'How should I know when I've never tried?' said Pippi. 'I've never had a piano to practise on, and I tell you, Tommy, to play the piano without having a piano needs a lot of practice.'

There was no piano shop in sight. Instead the children saw a chemist's. A large jar of freckle cream stood in the window, and beside the jar was an advertisement, saying: DO YOU SUFFER FROM FRECKLES?

'What does it say?' asked Pippi.

She could not read much, because she never wanted to go to school like other children.

'It says: "Do you suffer from freckles?"' said Annika.

'Oh, does it?' said Pippi thoughtfully. 'Well, a polite question should have a polite answer. Come along, let's go in!'

She pushed the door open and walked in, closely followed by Tommy and Annika. An elderly lady was standing behind the counter. Pippi went straight up to her.

'No,' she said firmly.

'What do you want, dear?' said the lady.

'No,' said Pippi again.

'I don't know what you mean,' said the lady.

'No, I do *not* suffer from freckles,' said Pippi.

Then the lady understood, but, glancing at Pippi, she exclaimed:

'But, my dear child, your face is full of freckles!'

'Of course,' said Pippi, 'but I don't suffer from them. I like them! Good morning!'

She started to walk out, but in the doorway she turned round and called:

'But if you get any cream that makes *more* freckles, send me about seven or eight jars.'

Next to the chemist's there was a shop which sold ladies' clothes.

'We haven't done much shopping yet,' said Pippi. 'We really must get down to it.'

They walked in, first Pippi, then Tommy, and then Annika. The first thing that caught their eye was a very elegant dummy in a blue silk dress. Pippi went up to the figure and grasped its hand cordially.

'How do you do?' she said. 'I suppose you're the lady who owns this shop. Pleased to meet you,' she said, shaking the dummy's hand even more vigorously.

But then something awful happened. The

figure's arm came loose and slid out of its silk covering, and there was Pippi with a long white arm in her hand. Tommy caught his breath in dismay, and Annika nearly burst into tears. The assistant rushed forward and began to scold Pippi dreadfully.

'Keep your hair on,' said Pippi when she got tired of listening. 'Isn't it self service here, then? I was thinking of buying this arm, you see.'

The assistant became angrier still, and said that the dummy was not for sale. In any case an arm could not be sold by itself, but Pippi would certainly have to pay the cost of the whole dummy, since she had broken it.

'That's queer,' said Pippi. 'It's a good thing they don't treat you like this in every shop. Suppose, next time I want to have pork chops for dinner, the butcher makes me buy a whole pig!'

While speaking she pulled out a couple of gold coins with a flourish from her apron pocket and threw them down on the counter. The assistant was thoroughly taken aback.

'Does the female cost more than that?' asked Pippi.

'Oh no, indeed not. It doesn't cost anything like so much,' answered the assistant very politely.

'Keep the change, then, and buy your children

some sweets with it,' said Pippi, moving towards the door. The assistant ran after her, asking respectfully to what address he might have the dummy sent.

'All I want is this arm, and I'll take it with me,' said Pippi. 'You can give the rest to the poor. Goodbye.'

'What *are* you going to do with that arm?' asked Tommy curiously, when they were out in the street again.

'Oh *that*,' said Pippi. 'What am I going to do with it? Haven't some people false teeth and false hair? Even false noses, sometimes. So why shouldn't I have one small false arm? Besides, I can tell you, it's jolly useful having three arms. I remember once when I sailed with Daddy on the high seas coming to a town where everyone had three arms. Not bad, eh? Just imagine! When they were eating, with a fork in one hand and a knife in the other, and suddenly they wanted to scratch their noses or ears, then it wasn't such a bad idea to get out the third arm. They saved a lot of time that way.'

Pippi looked thoughtful.

'Oh, dear me, I'm telling fibs,' she said. 'Queer, how suddenly such a lot of tales bubble up in me, and I can't help it. They didn't really have three arms at all in that town. Only two.'

She was silent for a moment, thinking.

'In fact, quite a lot of them only had one,' she said, 'and to tell the whole truth, there were even people who had none, and when they wanted to eat they had to lie down and lap from the plate. They couldn't scratch their own ears at all, they had to ask their mothers to do it for them.'

Pippi shook her head sadly.

'The fact is that I've never seen so few arms anywhere as in that town, but it's just like me: I'm an awful swank, trying to be important, and pretending that people have more arms than they really have.'

Pippi marched on with the false arm slung jauntily across her shoulder. She stopped at a sweet shop. A group of children was outside, gazing at all the wonderful things displayed in the window: large jars full of red and blue and green sweets, long rows of chocolate bars, piles and piles of chewing gum, and the most tempting toffee lollipops. No wonder the little children gazed and now and then heaved a heavy sigh, because they had no money, not even one little penny.

'Pippi, shall we go in?' said Tommy, eagerly tugging at Pippi's dress.

'We're *going* into this shop,' said Pippi. '*Far* into it!'

And they entered.

'Please may I have thirty-six pounds of sweets,' said Pippi, waving a gold coin in the air. The assistant only gaped. She was not used to anyone buying so many sweets at one time.

'You mean you want thirty-six sweets,' she said.

'I mean that I want thirty-six *pounds* of sweets,' said Pippi. She put the gold coin on the counter. The assistant hurriedly began pouring sweets into large bags. Tommy and Annika pointed to the sweets they thought the best. There were some red ones which were delicious; when you had sucked them for a while a lovely soft mixture oozed out. There were some green acid drops that were not bad either. The jelly babies and liquorice allsorts were jolly good, too.

'Let's have six pounds of each,' suggested Annika. And they did.

'Then if you give me sixty lollipops and seventy-two small packets of toffee, I don't think I need to take more than one hundred and three chocolate cigarettes for today,' said Pippi, 'except perhaps a small cart to carry them in.'

The assistant said she thought a cart could be bought at the toy shop close by.

By this time a lot of children had gathered outside the sweet shop. They were all staring through the window and gasped when they saw Pippi's way of doing her shopping. Pippi hurried into the toy shop, bought a cart, and loaded it with all the bags of sweets. She looked round and called out:

'Is there a child here who does *not* eat sweets? If so, will he or she please step forward.'

No one stepped forward.

'Strange!' said Pippi. 'Does there happen to be a child who *does* eat sweets, then?'

Twenty-three came forward, Tommy and Annika with them, of course.

'Tommy, open the bags!' said Pippi.

Tommy did so. A sweet-eating began, the like of which had never been seen in the little town. All the children filled their mouths with sweets, the red ones with the luscious juice inside, and the green acid ones, and the liquorice allsorts, and the jelly babies—all higgledy-piggledy. You could also have a chocolate cigarette in the corner of your mouth, because the taste of chocolate and jelly mixed was very nice. More children came running from every direction, and Pippi shared out handfuls all round.

'I think I shall have to buy another thirty-six pounds,' she said, 'otherwise there won't be anything for tomorrow.'

Pippi bought another thirty-six pounds, but

there was not much left for tomorrow in spite of it.

'Now we'll go to the next shop,' said Pippi and stalked into the toy shop. All the children followed. There were lots of nice things in the toy shop: trains and cars that could be wound up, pretty little dolls in beautiful dresses, dolls' china, and toy pistols, and tin soldiers, and soft toy dogs and elephants, and bookmarks, and jumping-jacks . . .

'Can I help you?' said the assistant.

'I'd like some of everything,' said Pippi, examining the shelves. 'We need, for instance, jumping-jacks and toy pistols,' she continued, 'but that can easily be put right, I expect.'

As she spoke Pippi pulled out a whole handful of gold coins, and then the children had to point out what they thought they needed most. Annika decided on a doll with fair, curly hair and a pink silk dress which could say 'mama' when you pressed its tummy. Tommy wanted a toy gun and a steam engine—and got them. All the other children pointed at what they wanted, and when Pippi had finished buying there was not much left in the shop, except for a few bookmarks and some building blocks. Pippi did not buy a single thing for herself, but Mr Nelson got a mirror.

Just before they left, Pippi bought each child a

toy ocarina, and when they were all out in the street again they played their ocarinas while Pippi beat time with the false arm. One little boy complained that his instrument would not work. Pippi took a look at it.

'No wonder, when there's chewing gum in it! Where did you pick up this treasure?' she asked, throwing away the large white ball. 'I don't remember buying any chewing gum.'

'I've had it since last Friday,' said the boy.

'Aren't you afraid your lips will grow together? That's what I thought usually happened to chewing gum chewers.'

She gave the boy back his ocarina, and he blew it merrily with the rest. There was such a noise in the High Street that at last a policeman came to see what was going on.

'What's all this?' he shouted.

'It's the Regimental March of the Grenadiers,' said Pippi, 'but I'm not sure all the children realize it. Some of them seem to think we're playing "Out roared the Dreadful Thunder".'

'Stop it!' yelled the policeman, covering his ears with his hands. Pippi patted him soothingly on the back with the false arm.

'You can thank your lucky stars we didn't buy trumpets,' she said.

One by one the ocarinas stopped playing.

Finally it was only Tommy's that gave a little squeak now and then. The policeman told them sternly that crowds were not allowed to collect in the High Street, and that the children must go home at once. The children did not mind. They were anxious to try out their toy trains and drive their motor-cars and make up the beds for their new dolls, so they all went home, happy and contented. They could not be bothered with supper that day.

It was time for Pippi and Tommy and Annika to go home, too. Pippi pulled the truck. She noticed all the shop signs as she passed them, and tried to spell as well as she could.

'*Apu-the-ca-ry*. Goodness! Isn't that where you buy meducin?' she asked.

'Yes, that's where you buy *medicine*,' said Annika.

'Ooh, then I must go in straight away and buy some,' said Pippi.

'But you're not ill,' said Tommy.

'I may not be ill now,' said Pippi, 'but I'm not taking any chances. Every year masses of people are taken ill and die, all because they didn't buy meducin in time: you bet I'm not going to be caught out that way.'

The apothecary was rolling pills, but he intended to roll only a few more because it was late, and near closing time. Then Pippi and Tommy and Annika walked up to the counter.

'Please can I have six pints of meducin?' said Pippi.

'What kind?' asked the apothecary impatiently.

'Well,' said Pippi, 'one that's good for illness.'

'What kind of illness?' asked the apothecary, still more impatiently.

'I think I'd like one that's good for whooping cough and blisters on the feet and tummy-ache and German measles and a pea that's got stuck in the nose, and all that kind of thing. It wouldn't be a bad idea if it could be used for polishing furniture as well. A real meducin, that's what I want.'

The apothecary said that no medicine was quite like that. There were different kinds of medicine for different illnesses, he explained, and when Pippi had mentioned about ten other complaints which she also wanted cured, he put a row of bottles on the counter. On some of them he wrote, 'Not to be taken,' which meant that the medicine was only meant to be applied to the skin. Pippi paid, took her bottles, thanked him and walked out. Tommy and Annika followed her. The apothecary looked at the clock and saw that it was time to close the shop. He locked the door carefully after the children and thought how nice it would be to go home to a meal.

Pippi put her bottles down on the doorstep.

'Oh, dear me,' she said. 'I nearly forgot the most important thing.'

As the door was now shut, she put her finger on the bell and rang long and hard. Tommy and Annika heard the shrill sound inside the shop. Presently a small window in the door was opened; this was the window through which you could buy medicine for people who fell ill at night. The apothecary popped his head out. His face was rather red.

'What do you want now?' he asked Pippi in a gruff voice.

'Please, Mr Aputhecary,' said Pippi, 'I've just thought of something. You know all about illness: what's really best for a tummy-ache? To eat black pudding or to put the whole tummy to soak in cold water?'

The apothecary's face became redder still.

'Be off with you, this very instant,' he shouted, 'or else . . . !'

He shut the window with a bang.

'Goodness, he's bad-tempered,' said Pippi. 'You'd almost think I'd annoyed him.'

She rang the bell again, and it was not many seconds before the apothecary's head appeared once more in the window. His face was as red as a beetroot.

'Black pudding is perhaps a little indigestible?' suggested Pippi, looking up at him with friendly eyes.

The apothecary made no reply, but simply slammed the window shut.

'Very well, then,' said Pippi, shrugging her shoulders, 'I'll just have to try black pudding, that's all. He'll only have himself to blame if it does me harm.'

She calmly sat down on the steps outside the shop and arranged all her bottles in a row.

'My goodness, how unpractical grown-ups can be!' she said. 'There are—let's see—eight bottles, and one bottle would easily hold the lot. Lucky I've got some commonsense myself,' and she uncorked the bottles and emptied all the medicine into one of them. She shook it vigorously, and raising it to her mouth, she drank a large dose. Annika, knowing that some of the medicine was meant for putting on the skin, was rather worried.

'Oh, Pippi,' she said, 'how do you know that the medicine isn't poisonous?'

'I shall find out,' said Pippi gaily. 'I shall find out tomorrow at the latest. If I'm still alive then, it's not poisonous, and the smallest child can drink it.'

Tommy and Annika considered this. After a while Tommy said doubtfully, and rather dolefully:

'Yes, but supposing it is poisonous, after all, what then?'

'Then you'll have to use what's left over for polishing the dining-room furniture,' said Pippi, 'and poisonous or not, the meducin won't be wasted.'

She took the bottle and placed it on the cart. It already contained the false arm, and Tommy's steam engine and toy gun, and Annika's doll, and a bag with five small sweets which was all that was left of the two thirty-six pounds. Mr Nelson was sitting in it, too. He was tired, and wanted to go home.

'Besides, I can tell you, I think it's a jolly good meducin. I feel better already. I feel terrifically well, and fit for anything,' said Pippi, marching along jauntily. Off she went, with the cart, back to Villekulla Cottage. Tommy and Annika walked beside her feeling just a little queer in the tummy.

3
Pippi writes a Letter and goes to School

'Today,' said Tommy, 'Annika and I have written to our granny.'

'Have you?' said Pippi, while stirring the contents of a saucepan with an umbrella handle. 'I'm going to have a lovely dinner,' she said, sniffing the mixture. ' "Boil for an hour, stirring vigorously, serve immediately without ginger."—What was that you said? You've written to your granny, have you?'

'Yes,' said Tommy from his place on Pippi's

wood-box, where he sat with his legs dangling. 'We're sure to have an answer soon.'

'I never have any letters,' said Pippi ruefully.

'But you don't write any,' said Annika. 'If you don't write, of course you don't get any letters. And that's because you don't want to go to school. You can't learn to write if you don't go to school.'

'I *can* write,' said Pippi. 'I know a whole lot of letters. Fridolf, who was mate in my father's ship, taught me heaps, and when you're short of letters, you can always make it up with numbers. Of course I can write! But I don't know what to write about. What sort of thing do they usually put in letters?'

'Well,' said Tommy, 'first I ask Granny how she is, and then I tell her that I'm well. Then I talk a little about the weather and things like that. Today I also said that I had killed a large rat in our cellar.'

Pippi stirred and thought.

'It's hard luck on me not having any post. Everyone else has letters. This can't go on. Even if I haven't a granny to write to me, I can jolly well write to myself. I'm going to do it straight away.'

She opened the oven door and looked in.

'There should be a pen in here if I'm not mistaken.'

There was a pen in there. Pippi got it out. Then she tore up a large white paper bag and sat down at the kitchen table. She frowned deeply and looked very thoughtful.

'Don't disturb me, I'm thinking,' she said.

Tommy and Annika decided to play with Mr Nelson. They took it in turns to put on and take off his small suit. Annika also tried to tuck him up in the green doll's bed which was his. She wanted to play nurse. Tommy was to be the doctor, and Mr Nelson the sick child, but he *would* wriggle out of the bed and jump up and hang from the lamp. Pippi glanced up from her writing.

'Silly Mr Nelson,' she said. 'Sick children mustn't hang by their tail from the lamp. At least not in this country. I've heard, though, that it does happen in South Africa. They hang up the children from the lamp as soon as they have the slightest temperature, and there they have to stay until they're well again. But we're not in South Africa now!'

Finally Tommy and Annika left Mr Nelson and began to groom the horse. The horse was very pleased when they came out in the porch to him. He sniffed their hands to see if they had brought any sugar. They hadn't got any, but Annika went inside immediately and fetched a couple of lumps.

Pippi kept writing and writing. At last the letter was ready. She had no envelope, but Tommy ran home for one. He gave her a stamp as well. Pippi wrote her name and address carefully on the outside: 'Miss Pippilotta Longstocking, Villekulla Cottage.'

'What does it say in the letter?' asked Annika.

'How should I know?' said Pippi. 'I haven't had it yet.'

Just then the postman passed Villekulla Cottage.

'I'm in luck,' said Pippi. 'Fancy finding a postman just when I was wanting one.'

She ran out into the road.

'Please take this letter to Pippi Longstocking at once,' she said. 'It's urgent!'

The postman looked first at the letter, and then at Pippi.

'Aren't you Pippi Longstocking?' he said.

' 'Course, who did you think I was? The Empress of Abyssinia?'

'Why don't you take the letter, then?' said the postman.

'Why don't I take the letter? Should I take it myself? That's some cheek! So people should deliver their own letters nowadays, should they? And what are postmen for, I wonder? They might as well all be done away with. I never heard anything so foolish! No, my boy, if that's how you do your job, you'll never be a postmaster, mark my words!'

The postman thought he had better do what she asked. He went up and put the letter in Villekulla Cottage's letterbox. No sooner had it dropped into the box than Pippi fetched it out in great excitement.

'Ooh,' she exclaimed to Tommy and Annika, 'I can't wait to see what's in it! It's the first letter I've ever had!'

All three children sat down on the porch steps while Pippi tore open the envelope. Tommy and Annika read over her shoulder. This is what it said:

DEER PIPPI U R NOT ILL I HOP IT WOOD B 2 SAD IF U WARE ILL I AM WELL NUFFING RONG WITH THE WETHER HEAR YESTERDAY TOMY KILLD A LARG RAT

LUV FROM PIPPI

'Oh,' said Pippi, delighted, 'my letter is just like the one you wrote to your granny yesterday, Tommy. That shows it's a proper letter. I shall keep it all my life.'

She put the letter back in the envelope and stowed it away in one of the small drawers of the big cupboard which she had in the parlour. There was hardly anything that Tommy and Annika enjoyed so much as looking at all the lovely things in Pippi's cupboard. Very often Pippi gave them a little present, but there was no end to the things in the drawers.

'But, Pippi,' said Tommy, when she had put the letter away, 'there were rather a lot of spelling mistakes in it.'

'Yes, you really *should* go to school and learn to write a bit better,' said Annika.

'Thank *you*,' said Pippi. 'I did it once, for a whole day, and I got so much learning into my head that it's still swimming about in it.'

'We're having an outing any day now,' said Annika, '—the whole class.'

'Gosh,' said Pippi, chewing one of her plaits. 'Gosh! And I can't go, I s'pose, 'cos I don't go to school. People seem to think they can treat you anyhow just because you don't go to school and learn pluttification.'

'Multiplication,' said Annika firmly.

'That's what I said—pluttification.'

'We're going to walk six miles, far into the forest, and there we're going to play games,' said Tommy.

'Gosh,' repeated Pippi once more.

The following day was so warm and sunny that the children at school in the little town found it difficult to sit still at their desks. The teacher opened all the windows and let the sunshine stream in. There was a birch tree just outside the school and at the top of it sat a small starling, chirruping so merrily that Tommy and Annika and the others in the form could not help listening to him, and did not care at all about nine times nine making eighty-one.

Tommy suddenly jumped high in surprise.

'Look, ma'am,' he shouted, pointing through the window, 'there's Pippi!'

The eyes of every child were turned in the same direction. Yes! There was Pippi, sitting on a branch of the birch tree. She was quite close to the window, because the branch nearly touched the window edge.

'Hello, ma'am,' she shouted. 'Hello, everybody!'

'Good morning, Pippi,' said the teacher. Pippi had once come to school for a whole day, so the teacher knew her quite well. Pippi and the teacher had agreed that perhaps Pippi would come back one day when she was a little older and more sensible.

'What do you want, Pippi dear?' said the teacher.

'Well, I thought I'd ask you to throw me a little pluttification through the window,' said Pippi, 'just enough so that I can come on the outing. If you've thought out any new letters, would you throw them as well at the same time?'

'Wouldn't you like to come in?' asked the teacher.

'I'd rather not,' said Pippi honestly, as she leant back comfortably on the branch. 'It only makes me dizzy. It's so thick with learning in there that you can cut it with a knife. But don't you think,' she went on hopefully, 'that a little learning flies out through the window and settles on me—just enough for me to come on the outing?'

'Maybe,' said the teacher, and continued the arithmetic lesson. All the children thought it was nice to have Pippi sitting in the tree outside. She had given all of them sweets and toys on the day when she visited the shops. Pippi had Mr Nelson with her, of course, and the children were very amused to see the way he threw himself from one branch to another. Sometimes he jumped down to the window, too, and once took a great leap right on to Tommy's head, and started to scratch his hair. Then the teacher told Pippi that she must call Mr Nelson, because Tommy had to divide three hundred and fifteen by seven, and it could not be done with a monkey in one's hair. It seemed impossible to keep on with the lesson. The spring sunshine, and the starling, and Pippi, and Mr Nelson—it was all too much for the children.

'I do believe you are quite out of your senses, children,' said the teacher.

'Yes,' said Pippi from the tree, 'honestly, this doesn't seem quite the right kind of day for pluttification.'

'We are doing division,' said the teacher.

'On this sort of day there shouldn't be any kind of "tion" at all,' said Pippi, 'at least, not anything except jollification.'

The teacher gave up the struggle.

'Perhaps you can supply the jollification, then,' she said.

'Oh, I'm not specially good at jollification,' said Pippi, hanging upside down from the branch by her knees, so that her red plaits almost trailed on the ground, 'but I know of a school where they have nothing else except jollification. "All day Jollification" it says on the time-table.'

'Really,' said the teacher. 'And where is that school?'

'In Australia,' said Pippi, 'in a village in Australia—in the south.'

She pulled herself upright on the branch, and her eyes began to shine.

'What do they do when they have jollification?' asked the teacher.

'Oh, all sorts of things,' said Pippi. 'They usually start by jumping through the window one after the other. Then they give a terrific roar and rush into the classroom again and hop around on the desks until they're tired.'

'And what does the schoolmistress say to that?' asked the teacher.

'Oh her,' said Pippi. 'She hops, too, with the best of them. Then the children fight for half an hour or so. The teacher cheers them on. If it's raining, all the children take their clothes off and run outside and dance and jump in the rain. The teacher plays a march on the organ to help them keep the time. Some of them stand under the gutter pipe to get a good shower.'

'I see,' said the teacher.

'Yes-s,' said Pippi, 'and it's a frightfully good school, one of the best in Australia—but it's very far south.'

'I can imagine that,' said the teacher. 'I don't think we are going to have quite such a jolly time in this school, though.'

'Pity,' said Pippi. 'If it had only been a matter of hopping on the desks, I might have ventured in for a while.'

'You will have to put off the hopping until we have our outing,' said the teacher.

'Then I *really* can come?' shouted Pippi joyously

so that she turned a back somersault and fell from the tree. 'I shall write and tell them that in Australia, and they can keep their old jollification as far as I'm concerned, because an outing is miles better.'

4

Pippi goes on a School Outing

There was a sound of the tramping of many feet on the road, and lots of chattering and laughter. Tommy with a rucksack on his back, and Annika in a brand new cotton dress, and the teacher, and all the other boys and girls in the class were there except one poor child who had developed a sore throat on the very day of the outing. In front of them all rode Pippi on her horse. Behind her sat Mr Nelson with his pocket mirror in his hand. He caught the sunlight in it, and looked full of glee when he succeeded in dazzling Tommy with the reflection.

Annika had been quite sure it would rain on this day. She had been so sure of it that she nearly felt angry beforehand. But no, they were lucky; the sun kept shining from sheer force of habit, although it was the day of the outing, and Annika's heart leapt for joy as she walked along the road in her brand new cotton dress. All the children, for that matter, looked very happy and eager. Along the roadside there were baby willows, and once they passed a whole field full of cowslips. They all decided they would pick a bunch of willow and a big posy of cowslips on the way home.

'Isn't it a lovely, lovely day?' sighed Annika, looking up at Pippi who sat straight as a general on her horse.

'Yes, isn't it? I haven't had such fun since I fought a boxer in San Francisco,' said Pippi. 'Would you like a little ride?'

Annika said she would love it, and Pippi lifted her up and put her in front of herself on the horse, but when the other children saw this, they wanted rides, too, of course. So one after the other they had a ride, but Annika and Tommy had just a *little* longer than the rest. One girl had a sore foot, and Pippi let her sit behind her all the time, but Mr Nelson kept pulling her plait.

They were on their way to a forest which is called Monster Forest, because it is monstrously beautiful. When they were nearly there, Pippi jumped from the saddle, patted her horse, and said:

'Now you've carried us a long way, you must be tired. It isn't fair that one should do all the work.'

She lifted the horse in her strong arms and carried him all the way to a little glade in the forest where the teacher had called a halt. Pippi looked all round and shouted:

'Come on, you monsters, all of you! We'll see who's the strongest!'

The teacher explained that there were no monsters in the forest. Pippi was very disappointed.

'A Monster Forest without monsters! What will they think of next! Soon, I s'pose there'll be fires without fire, and Christmas parties without Christmas trees. It's jolly mean! The day they start having sweet shops without sweets I'll give them a piece of my mind. Well, there's nothing for it but to be a monster myself.'

She uttered such a terrifying roar that the teacher had to cover her ears, and several of the children were frightened out of their wits.

'Yes, let's pretend Pippi's a monster!' shouted Tommy in delight, clapping his hands. The children all thought this an excellent idea. The monster settled in a deep crevice in a rock which was to be its den. The children ran around outside, teasing it with shouts of:

'Silly, silly monster! Silly, silly monster!'

At this the monster rushed out uttering fierce howls, and chased the children who scattered in all directions to hide. Those who were caught were dragged into the hollow, and the monster said they were going to be cooked for dinner: but sometimes they managed to escape when the monster was out chasing other children. This meant climbing up the steep rock which formed the wall of the crevice, and that was quite difficult; there was only a small pine tree to hang on to, and it was a problem to know where to find a foothold. It was very exciting all the same, and the children thought it was the best game they had ever played. The teacher lay on the grass reading a book and glanced at the children every now and then.

'That's the wildest monster I ever saw,' she murmured to herself.

It was. The monster jumped, and howled, and threw three or four boys over its shoulder at a time, and dragged them back to the hollow.

Sometimes it climbed the highest tree at a terrific speed and leapt from branch to branch just like a monkey: sometimes it threw itself on to the horse and caught up with some of the children who were trying to escape between the trees. When the horse came galloping near them, the monster bent down and lifted them up in front and rode like lightning back to the hollow, shouting:

'I'm going to cook you for my dinner!'

The children had such a wonderful time that they did not want to stop, but suddenly there was complete silence. When Tommy and Annika came running to see what was happening, they found the monster kneeling on the ground, looking very queer. It was watching something clasped in its hand.

'He's dead! Look! He's quite dead!' said the monster.

It was a baby bird that was dead. It had fallen from its nest and been killed.

'Oh, what a shame!' said Annika. The monster nodded.

'Pippi! You're crying!' said Tommy suddenly.

'Crying? Me!' said Pippi. ''Course I'm not crying.'

'But your eyes are red,' persisted Tommy.

'Red?' exclaimed Pippi, and borrowed Mr Nelson's mirror to have a look. 'Is that what you call red eyes? Then you should have been with me and Daddy in Batavia! There was an old man there who had such red eyes that the police wouldn't let him show himself in the streets!'

'Why?' asked Tommy.

'Cos people thought he was a stop signal, silly! The traffic came to a standstill when he turned up. Red eyes? Me? Don't you believe I'm crying because of a stupid little bird like that!' said Pippi.

'Silly, silly monster! Silly, silly monster!'

The children came running from all over the place to see what the monster was up to. They found it putting the stupid little bird very gently on a bed of soft moss.

'If I could, I would make you alive again,' said Pippi with a deep sigh. There followed a colossal roar.

'Now I'm going to cook you for dinner,' she shouted, and with shrieks of joy the children disappeared among the bushes.

There was a girl in the class whose name was Ulla. She lived close to Monster Forest. Ulla's mother had promised that she could invite the teacher and everyone in her class (and Pippi, too, of course) home for refreshments in the garden. So, when the children had played the monster game for a long time, and had climbed the rock, and sailed bark boats on a big puddle, and seen who were brave enough to jump from a high stone, Ulla said she thought it was time they went to her house and had some orange squash. The teacher, who had read her book from cover to cover, thought so, too. She gathered the children together, and they left Monster Forest.

On the road they came upon a man with a cart loaded with sacks. The sacks were heavy, and there were many of them. The horse was old and tired. Suddenly one of the wheels ran into the ditch. The man, whose name happened to be Flowergrove, got terribly angry. He blamed the horse, and got out his whip. The next moment he was beating the horse violently. The horse tugged and pulled, trying with all its might to bring the load on to the road again, but he could not do it. Flowergrove got angrier and angrier and whipped harder and harder. Just then the teacher caught sight of him and was very distressed to see the poor horse being beaten.

'How *can* you treat an animal like that?' she said to Flowergrove. Flowergrove stopped for a second and spat before he answered:

'It's none of your business,' he said. 'If you don't shut up, I might give you a taste of the whip, too, the whole lot of you.'

He spat again and raised the whip. The poor

horse trembled all over. Then a streak of lightning seemed to tear through the flock of children. It was Pippi. She was white about the nose. And when Pippi was white about the nose, she was angry—Tommy and Annika knew that. She made a dash straight for Flowergrove, caught hold of him round the waist, and threw him high in the air. When he fell, she caught him, and threw him up again: four times, five times, six times he flew through the air. Flowergrove could not think what was happening to him.

'Help! Help!' he shouted in terror. In the end he landed with a bump in the road. He had dropped his whip. Pippi stood beside him with her hands on her hips.

'You're not going to beat that horse any more,' she said firmly. 'You're not going to, d'you hear? Once down in Cape Town I met another man who beat his horse. He had such a very smart and grand uniform, and I told him that if he whipped his horse any more, I would beat him so hard there wouldn't be a single thread left of his grand uniform. Fancy! A week afterwards he whipped his horse again! Pity about that grand uniform, wasn't it?'

Flowergrove remained sitting in the road, completely stunned.

'Where are you going with the load?' asked Pippi.

It was a frightened Flowergrove who pointed to a cottage a little way along the road.

'Over there,' he said.

Pippi unharnessed the horse, which was still trembling from exhaustion and fear.

'There you are, horsie,' she said. 'Now we'll see what we can do for you!'

She lifted him up in her strong arms and carried him home to his stable. The horse looked just as surprised as Flowergrove.

The children and the teacher were waiting in the road for Pippi. Flowergrove was standing by his load, scratching his head, wondering how he would get it home. Then Pippi came back. She picked up one of the big, heavy sacks and put it on Flowergrove's back.

'That's right,' she said, 'now we shall see if you're as clever at carrying as you are at whipping.'

Pippi took the whip.

'Really I ought to thrash you a bit with this as you seem so fond of thrashing, but the whip is just about finished,' she said, breaking off a piece, 'in fact, quite finished, worse luck,' she said, breaking the whip into small pieces.

Flowergrove staggered away with the sack

without saying another word: he just groaned a bit. Pippi took hold of the shafts of the cart and pulled it home for Flowergrove.

'That's all right. That won't cost you anything,' she said when she had put the cart outside Flowergrove's stable. 'It's a pleasure, and the flight won't cost you anything, either.'

Off she went. Flowergrove stood staring after her for a long time.

'Long live Pippi!' cried the children when Pippi returned. The teacher was very pleased with Pippi, too, and praised her.

'You did right,' she said. 'We should be kind to animals—and to humans too, of course.'

Pippi sat on her horse, looking pleased.

'Well, you can't say I wasn't kind to Flowergrove,' she said, 'all that air travel free!'

'That's why we are *here*,' continued the teacher, 'to show kindness to others.'

Pippi stood on her head on the horse's back, waggling her legs.

'Ha-ha,' she said, 'and why did the others come here then?'

In Ulla's garden there was a big table, laden with so many buns and cakes that the children's mouths watered. They quickly sat down round the table. Pippi was at one end. She immediately stuffed two buns into her mouth. It made her look like one of those cherubs with bulging cheeks.

'Pippi,' said the teacher reproachfully, 'you must wait till you are asked.'

'Don't pother about me,' Pippi managed to splutter through the buns. 'I'm not fusshy about mannersh.'

Then Ulla's mother came up to her, holding in one hand a jug of orange juice, and in the other a jug of chocolate.

'Will you have orange or chocolate?' she asked.

'Orange *and* shocolate,' said Pippi. 'Orange on one bun and shocolate on the other.'

Without further ado she seized the two jugs from Ulla's mother and took a long drink from each of them.

'She's been away at sea all her life,' whispered the teacher by way of explanation to Ulla's mother, who looked rather surprised.

'I quite understand,' nodded Ulla's mother, and decided not to take any notice of Pippi's bad manners.

'Ginger nuts?' she asked, offering a plate of them to Pippi.

'Oh? I hope they taste better than they look!' said Pippi, grabbing a handful. Then she caught sight of some delicious looking pink cakes further down the table. She gave Mr Nelson's tail a little tug, and said:

'Look here, Mr Nelson, get me one of those pink things over there. You might as well take two or three while you're about it.'

Mr Nelson scampered along the table, spilling the orange juice from the glasses.

When the party was over and Pippi went up to thank Ulla's mother, she said, 'I hope you've had enough to eat, dear.'

'No, I haven't, and I'm still thirsty,' said Pippi, scratching her ear.

'Yes, I'm afraid it wasn't much of a party,' said Ulla's mother.

'Could have been better,' replied Pippi amiably.

The teacher made up her mind to have a little talk with Pippi about how to behave.

'Look here, Pippi, my dear,' she said kindly. 'I'm sure you want to be a real lady when you are grown-up.'

'Oh, you mean one of those people with a veil over the nose and three chins underneath,' said Pippi.

'I mean a woman who knows how to behave, and who is always polite and considerate. A real lady—isn't that what you want to be?'

'I'll think it over,' said Pippi, 'because, you see,

I'd nearly made up my mind to be a pirate when I'm grown-up.'

She stood deep in thought for a while.

'Don't you think I could be a pirate and a Real Lady at the same time? Because then . . . '

The teacher did not think that this was possible.

'Dear, dear, which shall I choose?' said Pippi unhappily.

The teacher said that whatever career Pippi chose to follow, it would not hurt her to learn a few manners. Pippi must never behave at the table as she had done that afternoon.

'To think that it should be so difficult to know how to behave,' sighed Pippi. 'Couldn't you tell me the 'portantest rules?'

The teacher did her best, and Pippi listened with interest. You must not help yourself before being asked, you must not take more than one cake at a time, you must not eat with your knife, you must not scratch yourself while talking to other people, you must not do this, and you must not do that. Pippi nodded thoughtfully.

'I'll get up an hour earlier every morning to practise so that I shall get the hang of it in case I decide not to be a pirate,' she said.

Now the teacher told the children it was time to leave and march home. They all lined up. Only

Pippi remained on the lawn. She had her head cocked on one side as if she was listening for something.

'What's the matter, Pippi dear?' asked the teacher.

'Please, ma'am,' said Pippi, 'may a Real Lady's tummy gurgle?'

She was silent again listening.

'Cos if not,' she said at last, 'I might as well make up my mind straight away to be a pirate.'

5
Pippi goes to the Fair

It was the day of the fair in the little town. Once a year they had a fair, and on each occasion the children in the little town were wild with joy that anything so exciting could happen. The town did not look its usual self at all on this day. There were crowds jostling everywhere, flags were hoisted, and the market-place was full of stalls where you could buy the most wonderful things. There was such a noise, and such a commotion that it was quite a thrill just to walk about in the streets. Best of all, down by the toll gate there was a big fairground with a merry-go-round, and rifle ranges, and a theatre, and all sorts of amusements. A menagerie, too: a menagerie with every kind of wild animal imaginable—tigers, and giant snakes, and monkeys, and sea lions. If you stood outside the menagerie, you could hear queerer growls and roars than you had ever heard in all your life. If you had any money, you could, of course, go in and see it all, too.

It was no wonder that Annika's hair ribbon seemed to quiver with excitement when she was dressed and ready in the morning of that day, or that Tommy nearly swallowed his breakfast whole in his haste. Tommy and Annika's mother asked her children if they would like to go to the fair with her. Tommy and Annika looked a little uncomfortable and said that if their mother did not mind, they would really rather go with Pippi.

'Because, you see,' explained Tommy to Annika as they shot through Villekulla Cottage's garden gate, 'it's sure to be much more fun with Pippi.'

Annika agreed.

Pippi was dressed, and waiting for them in the centre of the kitchen. She had at last found her big cartwheel hat—in the wood-shed.

'I quite forgot that I'd used it for carrying

wood the other day,' she said, pulling the hat down over her eyes. 'Don't I look grand?'

Tommy and Annika had to admit that she did. Pippi had blackened her eyebrows with coal and painted her mouth and nails with red paint. She had put on a very grand, long evening dress, which was cut so low at the back that her red bodice was showing. Her big black shoes could be seen below the hem, and they looked smarter than usual, because she had tied the green bows on to them which she only used on special occasions.

'I thought I ought to look a Real Lady when I'm going to the fair,' she said, tripping along as daintily as anyone can in such large shoes. She held up the hem of her skirt, and said at regular intervals in a voice which was quite different from her usual one:

'Delaightful! Delaightful!'

'What's delightful?' asked Tommy.

'Me,' said Pippi in a satisfied tone of voice.

Tommy and Annika thought *everything* delightful on the day of the fair. It was delightful to mix with the crowds in the streets, and to go from one stall to another in the market and look at all the things which were spread out. To celebrate, Pippi bought a red silk scarf for Annika, and Tommy received a peaked cap of a kind that he had always longed for but which his mother did not want him to have. At another stall Pippi bought two glass clocks. They were full of pink and white hundreds and thousands.

'You *are* kind, Pippi,' said Annika, hugging her clock.

'Oh, yes, delaightful,' said Pippi. 'Delaightful,' she said, holding up her skirt with an air of great elegance.

A long stream of people was pouring down towards the toll gate. Pippi, Tommy, and Annika followed.

'What a lovely noise!' said Tommy joyfully. The barrel organs were playing, and the merry-go-round was spinning round: people shouted and laughed. Arrow shooting and china breaking were in full swing. At the rifle ranges people jostled to show their skill at shooting.

'I'd like to have a closer look at that,' said Pippi, tugging Tommy and Annika with her to a rifle range. Just then there was no one at that particular rifle range, and the woman who was in charge of handing out rifles and taking the money was rather cross, and three children were not what she would choose for customers. She took no notice of them at all. Pippi looked at the targets with interest. They consisted of three paper figures painted blue, and each had a face as round as a ball. In the middle of the face was a very red nose. The nose was the bull's eye. If you could not manage to hit the nose, you should at least try to get somewhere near it. Shots that did not hit the face were not counted.

By and by the woman became annoyed at seeing the children standing there. She wanted customers who could shoot and pay.

'So you're still hanging around,' she said crossly.

'No,' said Pippi seriously, 'we're sitting in the market-place, cracking nuts.'

'What're you staring at?' said the woman still more crossly. 'Are you waiting for someone to come and shoot?'

'No,' said Pippi, 'we're waiting for you to start turning somersaults.'

However, at that moment a customer came along. He was an impressive-looking man with a gold chain across his waistcoat. He took hold of a rifle and weighed it in his hand.

'I might as well fire a few rounds,' he said, 'just to show how it should be done.'

He looked round to see if he had an audience, but there was no one near except Pippi and Tommy and Annika.

'Watch me, children,' he said, 'and I will give you a first lesson in the art of shooting. This is how it should be done!'

He lifted the rifle to his cheek and fired the first shot: it missed! The second shot also. The third and the fourth missed, too! The fifth hit one figure on the lower part of its chin.

'Rotten rifle,' said the impressive-looking man, and threw down the weapon. Pippi picked it up and loaded it.

'You are clever,' she said. 'Another time I shall do *exactly* as you've taught us, not like this!'

Bang, bang, bang, bang, bang! Five shots had hit a paper figure bang in the middle of its nose. Pippi handed a gold coin to the woman and walked away.

The merry-go-round was so splendid that Tommy and Annika caught their breath with delight when they saw it. There were black and white and brown wooden horses. They had real manes and looked almost alive. They had saddles and reins, too. You could choose whichever horse you wanted. Pippi spent a whole gold coin on tickets. She got so many that there was hardly enough room for them in her big purse.

'If I'd given them another gold coin, they'd probably have given me the whole roundabout thing,' she said to Tommy and Annika who were waiting for her.

Tommy chose a black horse and Annika a white one. Pippi sat Mr Nelson on one of the black horses that looked very wild. Mr Nelson immediately started to inspect its mane to see if it had fleas.

'Is Mr Nelson going on the merry-go-round too?' asked Annika in surprise.

''Course!' said Pippi. 'If I'd thought of it I would have brought my horse, too. He could have done with a bit of fun, and a horse riding on a horse—that would have been something very special in the horse line.'

As for herself, Pippi leapt into the saddle of a brown horse, and a moment later the merry-go-round started off to the music of a barrel organ playing the tune: 'Do you remember childhood's happy days with its fun and laughter?'

Tommy and Annika both thought it was wonderful to go on a merry-go-round. Pippi looked pleased too. She stood on her head on the horse, with her legs right up in the air. Her long evening dress fell down round her neck. All that the people standing round could see was a red bodice, a pair of green knickers, Pippi's long thin legs with one brown and one black stocking, and her big black shoes which waved playfully backwards and forwards.

'That's how it's done when a Real Lady goes on a merry-go-round,' said Pippi when the first turn was over.

The children stayed a whole hour on the merry-go-round, but in the end Pippi felt quite cross-eyed and said that she saw three merry-go-rounds instead of one.

'Then it's difficult to know which to choose,' she said, 'so I think we might as well go somewhere else.'

She had heaps of tickets left, and those she gave to some little children who were standing near, and had not had a ride, because they had no money for tickets.

Outside a tent nearby a man stood shouting:

'Another performance starting in five minutes! You must not miss this unique drama! *The Murder of the Countess Aurora, or Who is Creeping in the Bushes?*'

'If anyone's creeping in the bushes, we must find out who it is straight away,' said Pippi to Tommy and Annika. 'Let's go in!'

Pippi went up to the box-office.

'Can I go in half price if I promise to look with one eye only?' she enquired, with a sudden attack of economy.

The ticket lady would not hear of it.

'I don't see any bushes, and no one creeping in them, either,' said Pippi crossly when she and Tommy and Annika had placed themselves in the front row close to the curtain.

'It hasn't started yet,' said Tommy.

At that moment the curtain went up, and they could see the Countess Aurora pacing the floor of the stage, wringing her hands and looking very worried. Pippi followed it all with keen interest.

'I think she's unhappy about something,' she said to Tommy and Annika, 'or else she's got a safety-pin sticking into her.'

The Countess Aurora *was* unhappy. She raised her eyes to the ceiling and said in a plaintive voice:

'Is there anyone so unhappy as I? My children have been taken from me, my husband has disappeared, and I myself am surrounded by scoundrels and bandits who want to kill me.'

'This is terrible to hear,' said Pippi, and her eyes went rather red.

'I wish I were dead already,' cried the Countess Aurora.

Then Pippi burst into a flood of tears.

'Please don't say that!' she sobbed. 'Things will get better, you'll see. I'm sure the children will turn up, and perhaps you can have another husband. There are so ma-any me-en in the wo-orld,' she hiccuped between sobs.

Then the theatre manager came up to Pippi— he was the man who had been standing outside the tent, shouting—and said that if she did not stop all that noise, she would have to leave the theatre immediately.

'I'll try,' said Pippi, rubbing her eyes.

It was a terribly exciting play. Tommy kept turning his cap round and round and inside out from sheer nervousness, and Annika's hands were clasped tight. Pippi's eyes were wet and did not leave the Countess Aurora for a minute. Things were going from bad to worse for the poor Countess. There she walked in the palace garden, suspecting nothing. Suddenly there was a shriek. It came from Pippi. She had caught sight of a man behind a tree, and he was looking far from friendly. The Countess Aurora seemed to have noticed the rustling, too, because she said in a frightened whisper:

'Who is creeping in the bushes?'

'I can tell you,' said Pippi eagerly, 'it's a sly, horrid man with a black moustache. Hide in the wood-shed and lock the door, for goodness' sake!'

Now the theatre manager came up to Pippi and said that she must go at once.

'And leave the Countess Aurora alone with that ruffian? You don't know me!' said Pippi.

On the stage the play continued. Suddenly the horrid man rushed out of the bushes and threw himself at the Countess Aurora.

'Your last hour has come,' he hissed between his teeth.

'We'll see about that,' said Pippi taking a leap on to the stage. She seized the bandit round the waist and threw him into the audience. She was still weeping.

'How could you?' she sobbed. 'What've you got against the Countess, I'd like to know? Think of it! She's lost her children and her husband. She's quite al-o-o-one!'

She went up to the Countess who had collapsed on a garden seat.

'You can come and live with me at Villekulla Cottage if you like,' she said soothingly.

Sobbing loudly, Pippi stumbled out of the theatre, closely followed by Tommy and Annika—and by the theatre manager. He shook his fists at her. The people in the theatre, however, clapped their hands and thought it was a splendid performance.

When they were outside Pippi blew her nose loudly and said:

'My goodness, that was a sad affair! Let's do something to cheer ourselves up!'

'The menagerie!' said Tommy. 'We haven't been to the menagerie.'

So off they went. But first they visited a sandwich stall where Pippi bought six sandwiches for each of them, and three big bottles of fizzy lemonade.

'Cos crying always makes me hungry,' said Pippi.

In the menagerie there were lots of interesting things to see: elephants, and two tigers in a cage, and several sea lions who could play ball, a whole lot of monkeys, and a hyena, and two giant snakes. Pippi immediately took Mr Nelson to the monkey cage to say 'How-do-you-do' to his relations. There sat a sad-looking old chimpanzee.

'Now, come on, Mr Nelson,' said Pippi, 'say "How-do-you-do" nicely! I should think that's your grandfather's cousin's aunt's little third cousin!'

Mr Nelson raised his straw hat as politely as he could, but the chimpanzee could not be bothered to return his greeting.

The two giant snakes were in a big box. Once an hour they were taken out of the box by the beautiful snake charmer called Mademoiselle Paula, who showed them on a platform. The children were in luck. A performance was just about to begin. Annika was very much afraid of snakes, so she took firm hold of Pippi's arm. Mademoiselle Paula lifted up one of the snakes, a big horrible ugly thing, and laid it round her neck like a fur.

'It's a boa constrictor,' whispered Pippi to

Tommy and Annika. 'I wonder what the other one is.'

She went to the box and lifted out the other snake. It was bigger, and more horrible still. Pippi laid it round her neck just as Mademoiselle Paula had done with the other. Everyone in the menagerie gave a shout of terror. Mademoiselle Paula threw her snake into the box and rushed forward to save Pippi from certain death. The noise made Pippi's snake frightened and angry. He could not understand at all why he should be hanging round the neck of a little red-haired girl instead of round Mademoiselle Paula's which he was used to. He decided to give the red-haired girl something to remember, and he coiled his body round her in a grip which would have squeezed an ox to death.

'Don't you try that old trick on me!' said Pippi. 'I've met bigger snakes than you, you know—in Indo-China.'

She loosened the snake and put him back into his box. Tommy and Annika had turned pale.

'That was a boa constrictor, too,' said Pippi, fastening one of her suspenders which had come undone. 'Just what I thought!'

Mademoiselle Paula kept on scolding Pippi in some foreign language. Everyone in the menagerie heaved a deep sigh of relief, but they sighed too soon. This was obviously a day when anything might happen. Afterwards, no one knew how it occurred. The tigers had been fed with large chunks of red meat, and later the keeper swore that he had shut the door properly, but soon someone screamed in terror.

'There's a tiger loose!'

The yellow striped brute lay curled up outside the menagerie, ready to spring. People fled in all directions, but one little girl was squeezed into a corner close to the tiger.

'Don't move!' people shouted to her. They hoped the tiger would leave her alone if she stayed still.

'What are we to do?' they said.

'Run for the police!' suggested one.

'Call the fire brigade!'

'Fetch Pippi Longstocking!' said Pippi, and stepped forward. She crouched down a few yards from the tiger, calling out to him:

'Puss, puss, puss!'

The tiger gave a dreadful growl and showed his fearful teeth. Pippi raised a warning finger.

'If you bite me, I'll bite you, and no mistake,' she said.

The tiger leapt straight at her.

'What's the matter with you? Can't you take a joke?' said Pippi, flinging him away from her.

With a growling roar, which made everyone shiver all over, the tiger threw himself again at Pippi. It was evident that he meant to break her neck this time.

'Have it your own way,' said Pippi, 'but don't forget it was you that started it!'

With one hand she pressed the tiger's jaws together, and then she carried him tenderly in her arms back to the cage while she hummed a little tune:

'I love little pussy, her coat is so warm.'

For the second time everyone heaved a sigh of relief. The little girl who had squashed herself into the corner ran to her mother crying that she never wanted to go to a menagerie again.

The tiger had torn the hem of Pippi's dress. Pippi looked at the torn bits and said:

'Has anyone got a pair of scissors?'

Mademoiselle Paula had a pair. She was not cross with Pippi any more.

'Here you are, you brave leetle girl,' she said, handing Pippi the scissors. Pippi promptly cut the dress off short, well above the knees.

'Good,' she said, 'now I look even better with my dress cut low at the top and high at the bottom. No one could possibly look twice as elegant!'

She walked in such an elegant way that her knees knocked together at each step.

'Delaightful,' she said, as she walked along.

You would expect that things would have become quieter by this time, but fair days are never really quiet, and this day was no exception.

In the town there was a ruffian who was very strong. All the children were afraid of him, and not only the children, for that matter. Everyone was frightened of him. Even the police liked to keep out of the way when Laban, the ruffian, was on the warpath. He was not angry always, but only when he had been drinking beer. He had been doing so on that market day. He rolled along the High Street, shouting and roaring, and hitting out with his dreadful arms.

'Get out of my way!' he shouted. 'Here comes Laban!'

People pressed anxiously against the walls of the houses, and many of the children wept with fright. The police were nowhere to be seen. By degrees Laban made his way to the toll gate. He was a horrible sight with long black hair hanging over his forehead, a big red nose, and a yellow tooth sticking out of his mouth. The people who were gathered down by the toll gate thought he looked more horrible than the tiger.

A little old man stood at a stall, selling sausages. Laban stalked up to him, banged his fist down on the counter, and shouted:

'Give me a sausage! And be quick about it!'

'That'll be three pence,' the man said politely.

'So you expect to be paid for it, too?' said Laban. 'You should be ashamed of yourself when you've got the chance to sell to a fine gentleman like me, you old blockhead. Hand over another sausage.'

The old man said he would rather have the money first for the sausage that Laban had already had. Laban seized the old man and shook him by the ear.

'Give me another sausage,' he ordered. 'Quick!'

The old man did not dare to disobey, but the people round could not help muttering disapprovingly. One of them was even brave enough to say:

'It's a shame treating a poor old man like that!'

Laban turned round. He looked them over with bloodshot eyes.

'Did someone open his mouth?'

The people became frightened and started to go away.

'Stay where you are!' bawled Laban. 'If anyone moves I'll beat him to a jelly. Stay where you are, I said! Because now Laban is going to show you a thing or two.'

He seized a handful of sausages and started to play ball with them. He threw the sausages in the air and caught some of them with his hands, but dropped many of them on the ground. The poor old sausage man nearly wept. At that moment a small figure came forward out of the crowd.

Pippi stopped immediately in front of Laban.

'And whose little boy might this be?' she said quietly. 'And what has his mother to say to him about flinging his breakfast around?'

Laban uttered a terrible roar.

'Didn't I tell you to stay where you are, all of you?' he shouted.

'D'you always turn on the radio full blast?' asked Pippi.

Laban raised a threatening fist, shouting, 'Brat!!! Do I have to mash you into pulp to make you quiet?'

Pippi stood with her hands on her hips, watching him with interest.

'Now, what exactly was it you did with those sausages?' she said. 'Was this it?'

Throwing Laban high up in the air, she played ball with him for a minute or two. People cheered loudly, and the old sausage man clapped his small, wrinkled hands and smiled.

When Pippi had finished, it was a very frightened Laban who sat on the ground, looking about him, dazed.

'I think it's about time he went home,' said Pippi.

Laban had no objection to this.

'But first there's a number of sausages to pay for,' said Pippi.

Laban got up and paid for eighteen sausages. Then he left without saying another word. He never behaved in quite such a bullying fashion again.

'Three cheers for Pippi!' shouted the crowd.

'Hooray for Pippi!' said Tommy and Annika.

'We don't need a policeman in this town,' said one, 'so long as we have Pippi Longstocking.'

'No, we don't!' said another. 'She takes care of tigers and ruffians.'

''Course there must be a policeman,' said Pippi. 'Someone has to see that all the bicycles are wrongly parked properly.'

'Oh, Pippi, you're wonderful,' said Annika as the children marched home from the fair.

'Oh, yes! Delaightful,' said Pippi. She held up her skirt which already ended halfway up her legs. 'Absolutely delaightful.'

6

Pippi is Shipwrecked

Every day when school was finished
Tommy and Annika rushed over to
Villekulla Cottage. They did not even
want to do their prep. at home, but took their
books over to Pippi's.

'Good,' said Pippi. 'You sit here and work,
and perhaps a little learning will stick to me, too.
Not that I feel I need it, exactly, but I think
perhaps I can't become a Real Lady if I don't
learn how many hottentots there are in Australia.'

Tommy and Annika were sitting by the kitchen

table with their geography books open. Pippi was sitting cross-legged in the middle of the table.

'But supposing,' said Pippi, putting her finger on her nose in a thoughtful manner, 'supposing, just when I've learnt how many hottentots there are, one of them goes and gets pneumonia and dies! Then it's all been for nothing, and here I am, no more of a Real Lady than before.'

She thought hard.

'Someone ought to tell the hottentots to behave, so that your books don't go wrong,' she said.

When Tommy and Annika had finished their homework the fun began. If the weather was fine, they went in the garden, rode on the horse for a little or climbed up on the roof of the shed where they sat down to drink coffee, or else they climbed the old oak which was quite hollow, so that they could get right inside the trunk. Pippi said it was a very remarkable tree, because ginger beer grew in it. It must have been true, because each time the children climbed down into their hiding-place in the oak, there were three bottles of ginger beer waiting for them. Tommy and Annika could not understand where the empties went, but Pippi said that they faded away as soon as the ginger beer was drunk. A remarkable tree, Tommy and Annika thought.

'Sometimes bars of chocolate grow in it, but

only on Thursdays,' said Pippi, so Tommy and Annika were most particular about going there every Thursday to collect bars of chocolate. Pippi said that if only the tree was watered properly now and then, she thought they could get it to grow bread rolls as well, and perhaps even a sirloin of beef.

If it was rainy weather they had to stay indoors, and that was fun, too. They could look at all the fine things in Pippi's drawers, or they could sit in front of the stove and watch Pippi making waffles and roasting apples; or they might pop down into the big box where the firewood was kept and sit there, listening to Pippi's stories of exciting adventures from the time when she sailed the ocean.

'The storm was terrible,' Pippi would say. 'Even the fishes were seasick and wanted to go ashore. I saw, with my own eyes, a shark which was green in the face, and an octopus holding its forehead with all its many arms. Shocking storm, that.'

'Oh, weren't you frightened, Pippi?' asked Annika.

'Yes, supposing you'd been shipwrecked!' said Tommy.

'Well,' said Pippi, 'I've been shipwrecked—more or less—so many times it doesn't scare me.

It takes a lot more to do that. I wasn't frightened when the raisins blew out of the Spotted Dick while we were having dinner, nor when the false teeth blew out of the cook's mouth, either. But when I saw the ship's cat losing his fur and sailing off in the air towards the Far East with nothing on, I began to feel a bit queer.'

'I've got a book all about a shipwreck,' said Tommy. 'It's called *Robinson Crusoe*.'

'Oh, yes, it's awfully good,' said Annika. 'Robinson Crusoe came to a desert island!'

'Have you really been shipwrecked, Pippi?' asked Tommy, making himself comfortable in the wood-box. 'And on a desert island?'

'I should jolly well think so,' said Pippi emphatically. 'You would have to look hard before you could find anything as shipwrecked as me. Robinson, he's miles behind. I should think there are only about eight or ten islands in the Atlantic and the Pacific where I *haven't* landed after a shipwreck. They're on a special black list in the tourist handbooks.'

'It must be fun to be on a desert island!' said Tommy. 'I'd love it!'

'That's easily arranged,' said Pippi. 'There's no shortage of islands.'

'No,' said Tommy, 'I know of one not far from here.'

'Is it in a lake?' asked Pippi.

' 'Course,' said Tommy.

'Splendid!' said Pippi. 'Cos if it had been on dry land it wouldn't have been any good.'

Tommy was wild with excitement.

'Let's go!' he shouted. 'Straight away!'

In two days' time Tommy and Annika's summer holidays would begin. Then their mother and father were going away. They would never have a better chance to play Crusoe.

'To play shipwreck,' said Pippi, 'we must first have a boat.'

'And we haven't got one,' said Annika.

'I've seen an old broken rowing-boat at the bottom of the stream,' said Pippi.

'But it *has* been shipwrecked already,' said Annika.

'All the better,' said Pippi. 'Then it knows how to do it.'

For Pippi it was a simple matter to raise the sunken boat. She then spent all day on the bank of the stream making the boat water-tight, and the whole of a rainy morning she worked in the wood-shed making a pair of oars.

And then Tommy and Annika's summer holidays began, and their parents went away.

'We shall be back in two days' time,' said their mother. 'You must be very good and obedient, and remember to do exactly as Ella tells you.'

Ella was the maid, and she was supposed to look after Tommy and Annika while their mother and father were away. But when the children had been left alone with Ella, Tommy said:

'Ella, you needn't look after *us*, we shall be at Pippi's all the time.'

'Besides, why shouldn't we look after ourselves?' said Annika. 'Pippi *never* has anyone to look after *her*, so why shouldn't we be left in peace—for a couple of days, anyway?'

Ella had no real objection to a two days' holiday, and Tommy and Annika begged and prayed so hard that at last Ella agreed to go home and stay with her mother. But the children must promise faithfully to eat and sleep properly and not be out in the evening without a woolly on. Tommy said he would gladly wear a dozen jerseys if only Ella went.

So it was all settled. Ella went off, and two hours later Pippi, Tommy and Annika, the horse, and Mr Nelson began their journey to the uninhabited island.

It was a mild evening in early summer; the air was warm though the sky was cloudy. They had quite a long way to go before they reached the lake with the uninhabited island. Pippi carried the boat upside down on her head. She had packed an enormous sack and a tent on the horse's back.

'What's in the sack?' asked Tommy.

'Food and weapons and blankets and an empty bottle,' said Pippi. 'You see, I thought we'd have a fairly comfortable shipwreck as it's your first. Usually when I'm shipwrecked I always shoot an antelope or a llama and eat the meat raw, but there mightn't be any antelopes or llamas on this island, and it would be tiresome if we died of hunger because of such small details.'

'What are you going to do with the empty bottle?' asked Annika.

'What am I going to do with the empty bottle? What a silly question! A boat, of course, is the most important thing when you're going to be shipwrecked; but next comes an empty bottle. My father taught me that when I was in my cradle. "Pippi," he said, "it doesn't matter if you forget to wash your feet when you're going to be presented at Court, but if you forget the empty bottle when you're going to be shipwrecked you're done for."'

'Yes, but what's it for?' persisted Annika.

'Haven't you ever heard of bottle post?' said Pippi. 'You write a letter asking for help, then you put it into the bottle, push the cork in, and throw the bottle into the water, and it floats straight to someone who will come and save you. How else did you think you could survive a shipwreck? Leave everything to chance? Certainly not!'

'Oh, is that what you do?' said Annika.

Soon they arrived at a little lake, and there in the middle was the uninhabited island. The sun was just coming out from behind the clouds, casting a friendly glow over the pale green of the early summer landscape.

'Well,' said Pippi, 'if that isn't one of the nicest uninhabited islands I've ever seen!'

Quickly she heaved the boat into the lake, relieved the horse of his load and stowed it all in the bottom of the boat. Annika and Tommy and Mr Nelson jumped in. Pippi patted the horse.

'Dear old horsie, much as I'd like to, I can't invite you to come in the boat. I hope you can swim. It's as simple as anything. Watch me!'

She plunged into the water with her clothes on and did a few strokes.

'It's terrific fun, you know, and if you want more fun still, you can play whales. Like this!'

Pippi filled her mouth with water, lay floating on her back, and spouted like a fountain. The horse did not look as if he thought it was particularly amusing, but when Pippi went aboard, took the oars, and rowed off, the horse threw himself into the water and swam after her. But he did not pretend he was a whale. When they had nearly reached the island, Pippi shouted:

'All hands to the pumps!'

And a second later:

'In vain! Abandon ship! Everyone who can, save himself!'

She stood on the stern and threw herself head first into the water. Soon she was up again, caught hold of the painter and swam towards land.

'The provisions must be saved anyway, so the crew might as well stay on board,' she said. She made fast the boat to a stone and helped Tommy and Annika ashore. Mr Nelson managed to get ashore by himself.

'A miracle has happened,' shouted Pippi. 'We are saved. At least for the time being. Provided there aren't any cannibals and lions here.'

The horse had by now also reached the island. He stepped out of the water and shook himself.

'Oh, look, here's our first mate, too,' said Pippi, pleased. 'Let's hold a council of war!'

From the sack she brought out her pistol which she had once found in a sailor's chest in the attic of Villekulla Cottage. With the pistol cocked she crept cautiously forward looking in every direction.

'What's the matter?' said Annika anxiously.

'I thought I heard the growl of a cannibal,' said Pippi. 'You can't be too careful. It wouldn't be much use saving yourself from drowning only to be served with two vegetables as dinner for a cannibal!'

But there were no cannibals in sight.

'They've retreated and are lying in ambush,' said Pippi. 'Or else they're probably studying the cookery book to see how to cook us. And I must say that if they serve us with carrots and white sauce I shall never forgive them. I loathe carrots.'

'Pippi, don't talk like that,' said Annika shuddering.

'Oh! So you don't like carrots either? Well, anyway we'll start putting the tent up.'

This Pippi did, and soon it was pitched in a sheltered spot, and Tommy and Annika crawled in and out and were thrilled. A little distance from the tent Pippi laid a few stones in a ring and on these she put sticks and twigs which she gathered.

'Oh, how lovely to have a fire!' said Annika.

'Yes, rather!' said Pippi. She took two pieces of wood and started to rub them together. Tommy was very interested.

'Oh, Pippi,' he said in delight, 'you're making a fire like the cannibals do!'

'No, I'm warming my fingers,' said Pippi, 'and this is just as good as beating one's arms. Let me see now, where did I put that box of matches?'

Soon the fire was burning brightly, and Tommy said he thought it was very cosy.

' 'Tis, and keeps the wild animals away, too,' said Pippi.

Annika caught her breath.

'What wild animals?' she asked in a trembling voice.

'The mosquitoes,' said Pippi, thoughtfully scratching a big mosquito bite on her leg.

Annika heaved a sigh of relief.

'And the lions, too, of course,' continued Pippi. 'But it's not supposed to be any good against pythons or bisons.'

She patted her pistol.

'But don't worry, Annika,' she said. 'With this I'll manage all right, even if a field mouse should come.'

Then Pippi brought out coffee and sandwiches, and the children sat round the fire, eating and drinking and having a lovely time. Mr Nelson sat on Pippi's shoulder. He was eating, too. Every now and then the horse put his nose forward for a piece of bread and some sugar, and he also had lots of beautiful green grass to graze on.

There were clouds in the sky, and it was

becoming dark among the bushes. Annika moved as close to Pippi as she could get. The flames from the fire threw strange shadows. The darkness beyond the little circle of light from the fire seemed somehow alive.

Supposing there was a cannibal behind that juniper bush, or a lion hiding behind the big stone!

Pippi put her coffee cup down.

'Fifteen men on the Dead Man's Chest—
Yo-ho-ho, and a bottle of rum!'

she sang in a hoarse voice.

Annika shivered still more.

'That tune is in another of my books,' said Tommy eagerly. 'One about pirates.'

'Is it really?' said Pippi. 'Then it must be Fridolf that wrote the book, because he taught me the tune. Many a time I've sat on the afterdeck of my father's ship on starlit nights with the Southern Cross straight above my head and Fridolf beside me, and heard him sing like this:

'Fifteen men on the Dead Man's Chest—
Yo-ho-ho, and a bottle of rum!'

Pippi sang once more in a hoarser voice still.

'Pippi, it makes me feel very queer when you sing like that,' said Tommy. 'It's frightening and lovely all at the same time.'

'It's only frightening to me,' said Annika, 'but perhaps a little lovely, too.'

'I shall go to sea when I'm grown up,' said Tommy firmly. 'I shall be a pirate, just like you, Pippi.'

'Good!' said Pippi. 'The Terrors of the Caribbean Sea, that'll be you and me, Tommy. We shall make off with gold and jewels and precious stones and have a hiding-place for our treasures deep in a cave on a desert island in the Pacific, and three skeletons to guard the cave. We'll have a flag with a skull and two crossbones on it, and we'll sing "Fifteen men" so it can be heard from one end of the Atlantic to the other and all the seafarers will grow pale and think of throwing themselves into the sea to escape our bloody, bloody vengeance!'

'What about me?' said Annika plaintively. 'I'm afraid to be a pirate. What shall *I* do?'

'You can come all the same,' said Pippi, 'to dust the pianola!'

The fire was dying down.

'Time for bed,' said Pippi. She had laid branches of spruce on the floor of the tent and several thick blankets over the branches.

'Would you like to sleep like sardines with me in the tent?' said Pippi to the horse. 'Or would you rather stay out here under a tree with a horse blanket over you?—What was that you said?—You always feel sick sleeping in a tent. Just as you like,' and Pippi gave him a friendly pat.

Soon all three children and Mr Nelson were rolled in their blankets in the tent. Outside, the waves lapped against the shore.

'Hear the roar of the ocean,' said Pippi dreamily.

It was pitch dark, and Annika clutched Pippi's hand because everything seemed less dangerous then. Suddenly it started to rain. The drops splashed on the canvas, but inside the tent it was warm and dry. The sound of the rain outside made it seem all the cosier. Pippi went out to put another blanket on the horse. He was standing under a thick spruce, so he was all right.

'Isn't it grand?' sighed Tommy when Pippi returned.

'Rather,' said Pippi. 'And look what I found under a stone! Three bars of chocolate!'

Three minutes later Annika was fast asleep with her mouth full of chocolate and her hand in Pippi's.

'We've forgotten to brush our teeth,' said Tommy and fell fast asleep.

When Tommy and Annika woke up, Pippi had disappeared. Eagerly they crawled out of the tent. The sun was shining. A fresh fire was burning in front of the tent and Pippi was sitting by it frying bacon and making coffee.

'Happy Easter!' she said when she caught sight of Tommy and Annika.

'Easter?' said Tommy. 'It's not Easter!'

'Isn't it?' said Pippi. 'Well, save it up for next year then!'

The children sniffed the delicious smell from the bacon and the coffee. They squatted by the fire, and Pippi passed them bacon and eggs and potatoes. Afterwards they had coffee with ginger nuts. Never before had a breakfast tasted so good.

'I think we're better off than Robinson Crusoe,' said Tommy.

'Well, if we have a little fresh fish for dinner as well, you bet Robinson would be green with envy,' said Pippi.

'Ugh, I don't like fish,' said Tommy.

'I don't either,' said Annika.

Pippi, however, cut a long thin branch, tied a piece of string at one end, bent a pin into a hook, put a bread pellet on to the hook and sat herself on a big stone on the shore.

'Now we shall see what happens,' she said.

'What're you fishing for?' asked Tommy.

'Octopus,' said Pippi. 'It's a delicacy beyond compare.'

She sat there for a whole hour, but no octopus nibbled. A perch came up and nosed at the bread crumb, but Pippi quickly pulled up the hook.

'No, thank you, my boy,' she said. 'I said octopus, and I mean octopus, so it's no use you coming sponging.'

After a while Pippi threw the fishing rod into the lake.

'You were lucky that time,' she said. 'It looks like pancakes instead. The octopus is obstinate today.'

Tommy and Annika were well content. The water glittered invitingly in the sunshine.

'What about a swim?' said Tommy.

Pippi and Annika were all for it. The water was rather cold. Tommy and Annika dipped their big toes in, but quickly withdrew them.

'I know a better way,' said Pippi. There was a rock close to the water's edge, and on the rock grew a tree. The branches stretched out over the water. Pippi climbed the tree and tied a rope round a branch.

'Look!' She took hold of the rope, threw herself into the air and slid down into the water. 'This way you get wet straight away,' she shouted when she reached the surface.

Tommy and Annika were at first rather doubtful, but it looked such fun that they decided to have a go, and once they had tried it they did not want to stop. It was even more fun than it looked. Mr Nelson wanted to join in, too. He slid down the rope, but a second before he would have splashed in the water he turned round and started to climb up at a terrific speed. He did that each time although the children called to him that he was a coward. Pippi then hit upon the idea that they could sit on a plank of wood and slide on it down the rock into the water—and that was great fun, too, because there was such a tremendous splash when it reached the water.

'That chap Robinson, I wonder if he slid on a plank of wood,' mused Pippi when she sat at the top of the rock ready to start off.

'No-o—at least, it doesn't say so in the book,' said Tommy.

'That's what I thought. His shipwreck wasn't much to write home about, *I* don't think. What did he do with himself all day long? Sew cross-stitch? Yippy! Here goes!'

Pippi slid downwards, her red plaits flying.

After the bathe the children decided to explore the uninhabited island properly. They all three mounted the horse, and he trotted along good-naturedly. Up hill and down dale they went, through thickets and among dense spruce, over marsh land and across beautiful little glades where masses of wild flowers were growing. Pippi sat with her pistol at the ready, and now and then she fired a shot. This made the horse cut great capers with fright.

'There a lion bit the dust,' she said, pleased. Or:

'*That* cannibal has planted his last potato!'

'Let's keep this for our own island always,' said Tommy when they had returned to camp and Pippi had started making pancakes.

Pippi and Annika agreed.

Pancakes taste very good when you eat them smoking hot. There were no plates and no forks and knives handy, and Annika asked:

'Can we eat with our fingers?'

'I don't mind,' said Pippi, 'but myself, I'd rather stick to the old method of eating with my mouth.'

'You know what I mean,' said Annika. She picked up a pancake with her little hand and put it with great relish into her mouth.

Once more it was evening. The fire had been put out. Pressed against each other, their faces smeared with pancake, the children lay in their blankets. A big star shone through a slit in the tent canvas. The lapping of the water soothed them to sleep.

'We've got to go home today,' said Tommy gloomily next morning.

'It's an awful shame,' said Annika. 'I'd like to stay here all summer, but Mummy and Daddy are coming back today.'

After breakfast Tommy took a stroll down by the lake. Suddenly he gave a terrific yell. The boat! It was gone! Annika was very upset. How were they to get away now? It is true, she very much wanted to stay on the island for the whole summer but it was a different thing to know that you *could* not go home. And what would their poor mother say when she realized that Tommy and Annika had disappeared? Tears came into Annika's eyes as she thought of it.

'What's the matter with you, Annika?' said Pippi. 'What's your idea of a shipwreck, I'd like to know? What d'you think Robinson would have said if a ship had come to fetch him when he'd been on his desert island for two days? "Here you are, Mr Crusoe! Will you please go on board and be saved and bathed and shaved and have your toenails cut!" No, *thank* you! I'm pretty well sure Mr Crusoe would have run away and hidden behind a bush, because once you've managed to get to a desert island, you certainly don't want to stay less than seven years.'

Seven years! Annika shuddered, and Tommy looked very doubtful.

'Well, I don't mean that we're going to stay here for simply ages,' said Pippi reassuringly. 'When it's time for Tommy to do his National Service, I s'pose we've got to let them know where we are. But perhaps he can get a deferment for a year or two.'

Annika felt more and more desperate. Pippi looked at her thoughtfully.

'Well, if you're going to take it like that,' she said, 'I s'pose there's nothing for it but to send off the bottle.'

She went and dug out the empty bottle from the sack. She also managed to find a paper and pencil. She put them all on a stone in front of Tommy.

'You write,' she said. 'You're much more used to writing than me.'

'But what shall I write?' asked Tommy.

'Let's see,' said Pippi, thinking hard. 'Write: "Save us before we perish! For two days we have pined away without snuff on this island."'

'Pippi, we can't write that,' said Tommy reproachfully. 'It isn't true.'

'What isn't?' said Pippi.

'We can't write "without snuff",' said Tommy.

'Why not?' said Pippi. 'Have you got any snuff?'

'No,' said Tommy.

'Has Annika got any snuff?'

' 'Course not, but—'

'Have I got any snuff?' asked Pippi.

'P'raps not,' said Tommy, 'but we don't take snuff.'

'And that's exactly what I want you to write: "For two days without snuff . . ." '

'But if we write that I'm sure people will think we take snuff,' persisted Tommy.

'Look, Tommy,' said Pippi. 'Tell me this, who's without snuff *oftenest*? The ones that take it or the ones that don't take it?'

'The ones that *don't* take it, of course,' said Tommy.

'Well, what's all the fuss about then?' said Pippi. 'You're to write what I tell you!'

So Tommy wrote: 'Save us before we perish! For two days we have pined away without snuff on this island.'

Pippi took the paper, pushed it into the bottle, put the cork in, and threw the bottle into the water.

'Our rescuers should soon be here,' she said.

The bottle bobbed about, and soon it came to rest among the roots of an alder by the shore.

'We have to throw it further out,' said Tommy.

'That'd be the silliest thing to do,' said Pippi.

'If it floated far away, our rescuers wouldn't know where to look for us, but if it's here we can shout to them when they've found it, and we'll be saved immediately.'

Pippi sat down on the shore.

'We'd better keep our eye on the bottle all the time,' she said. Tommy and Annika sat down beside her. After ten minutes Pippi said impatiently:

'People seem to think we've got *nothing* else to do except sit and wait to be rescued. Where are they, I'd like to know?'

'Who?' asked Annika.

'The people who're going to rescue us,' said Pippi. 'The carelessness and negligence of it is quite shocking when you think that lives are at stake.'

Annika began to think that they were really going to pine away on the island, but suddenly Pippi put her finger up and shouted:

'Goodness me! What a scatterbrain I am! How *could* I forget?'

'What?' asked Tommy.

'The boat,' said Pippi. 'I carried it up on land last night when you'd gone to sleep. Now I remember.'

'But why?' said Annika reproachfully.

'I was afraid it might get wet,' said Pippi.

In a twinkling she had fetched the boat which

had been well hidden under a spruce. She heaved it into the lake and said grimly:

'There! Let 'em come! Cos when they come to rescue us, it'll be for nothing, cos we're going to rescue ourselves. That'll serve them right. It'll teach them to be quicker another time.'

'I hope we'll be home before Mummy and Daddy,' said Annika when they had got into the boat and Pippi was rowing with strong strokes towards land. 'Mummy will be terribly worried otherwise.'

'I don't think so,' said Pippi.

Mr and Mrs Settergreen did reach home half an hour before the children. There was no trace of Tommy and Annika. But in the letter-box they found a piece of paper, and on it was written:

DO NOT PINK YOR CHILREN DED OR DISAPPEERD FOR EVER COS THA ARNT ONLE A LITTL SHIPRECKD AND COMING HOM SOON I PROMMIS

LUV FROM PIPPI

7
Pippi has a Grand Visitor

One summer evening Pippi and Tommy
and Annika sat on Pippi's front doorstep eating wild strawberries which they
had picked that afternoon. It was such a lovely
evening with bird song and the scent of flowers
and—yes, the strawberries. It was all very
peaceful. The children ate and hardly talked at all.
Tommy and Annika sat thinking how lovely it
was that it was summer time and what a blessing
school would not be starting for a long time yet.
What Pippi was thinking no one knows.

'Pippi, you've been here at Villekulla Cottage for a whole year now,' said Annika suddenly, and squeezed Pippi's arm.

'Yes, time flies, and I'm getting old,' said Pippi. 'I shall be ten in the autumn and then I s'pose I shall be past my prime.'

'Will you live here always, d'you think?' asked Tommy. 'I mean, until you're big and old enough to be a pirate.'

'No one knows,' said Pippi, 'because I don't suppose my father will stay on that Cannibal Island for ever, and as soon as he's got a new boat ready I expect he'll come and fetch me.'

Tommy and Annika sighed. Suddenly Pippi sat bolt upright on the steps.

'Look! Why, there he is!' she said pointing down towards the gate. She was down the garden path in three leaps. After some hesitation Tommy and Annika followed and saw her throw her arms round the neck of a very fat man with a red, clipped moustache and wearing blue sailor's trousers.

'Darling Daddy!' shouted Pippi, waggling her legs so vigorously as she hung round his neck that her big shoes fell off. 'Daddy! How you have grown!'

'Pippilotta Provisiona Gaberdina Dandeliona Ephraims-daughter Longstocking, my darling child! I was just about to say that you have grown.'

'Ha-ha, I knew that!' laughed Pippi. 'That's why I said it first!'

'My child, are you as strong as you used to be?'

'Stronger,' said Pippi. 'Let's have a tug-of-war!'

'Right-o,' said her father.

There was only one person in the world as strong as Pippi, and that was her father. There they were, tugging with all their might, but neither succeeded in beating the other. At last, however, Captain Longstocking's arm began to tremble and Pippi said:

'When I'm ten, I'll get the better of you, Daddy.'

Her father thought so, too.

'But, goodness me,' said Pippi, 'I'm forgetting the introductions. This is Tommy and this is Annika. And this is my father, the sea captain and His Majesty Ephraim Longstocking—because you are a Cannibal King, aren't you, Daddy?'

'Exactly,' said Captain Longstocking. 'I'm the king of the Canny Cannibals of Canny-Canny Island. I floated ashore there after I'd been blown into the sea, you remember.'

'That's just what I thought,' said Pippi. 'I knew all along that you weren't drowned.'

'Drowned! 'Course not! It's as impossible for me to sink as for a camel to thread a needle. My fat keeps me afloat.'

Tommy and Annika looked at Captain Longstocking wonderingly.

'Why haven't you got any Cannibal King clothes on?' asked Tommy.

'They're here in my bag,' said Captain Longstocking.

'Put them on! Put them on!' shouted Pippi. 'I want to see my father in royal attire.'

They all went into the kitchen. Captain Longstocking disappeared into Pippi's bedroom, and the children sat down on the wood-box and waited.

'This is just like the theatre,' said Annika expectantly.

Then—bang—the door opened, and there stood the Cannibal King. He was wearing a straw skirt and on his head was a crown of gold. Round his neck there were strings and strings of beads. In one hand he was carrying two arrows and in the other a shield. And that was all. No, not quite; below the straw skirt his fat, hairy legs were decorated with gold rings round the ankles.

'Ussamkussor mussor filibussor,' said Captain Longstocking, puckering his eyebrows in a threatening manner.

'Ooh, he's talking cannibal language,' said Tommy delightedly. 'What does it mean, sir?'

'It means, "Tremble, my enemies!"'

'Daddy,' said Pippi, 'weren't the cannibals surprised when you floated ashore on their island?'

'Yes, they certainly were,' said Captain Longstocking, 'they were terrifically surprised. At first they thought they'd eat me up, but when I uprooted a palm tree with my bare hands they thought better of it, and made me king. So then I ruled in the mornings and worked at building my boat in the afternoons. It took me a long time to get it finished as I had to do it all myself. It was only a little sailing boat, of course. When I was ready I told the cannibals that I should have to leave them for a little time, but that I would soon return and then I would bring a Princess whose name was Pippilotta. Then they beat their shields and shouted, "Ussumlussor! Ussumplussor!"'

'What does that mean?' said Annika.

'It means, "Bravo! Bravo!" Then I ruled really strongly for a fortnight so that it would last for the whole time that I was going to be away, and then I hoisted the sail and made a bee-line for the open sea, and the cannibals shouted, "Ussumkura kussomkara!" That means, "Come back soon, fat white chief!" I set my course for Sourabaya, and what do you think was the first thing I saw when

I jumped ashore there? My staunch old schooner the *Hoppetossa* with my faithful old Fridolf standing by the rail waving for all he was worth. "Fridolf," I said, "I am back to resume command." "Aye, aye, Cap'n," he said. And I went on board. Every man of the old crew is still on it, and now the *Hoppetossa* is lying at anchor in the harbour here, so you can go and see all your old friends, Pippi.'

This made Pippi so happy that she stood on her head on the kitchen table and waggled her legs. But Tommy and Annika could not help feeling a little sad. They felt as if someone was taking Pippi away from them.

'This calls for a celebration!' shouted Pippi when she was on her feet again. 'A celebration that'll make the whole of Villekulla Cottage creak.'

So she laid a substantial supper on the kitchen table and they all sat down and ate. Pippi swallowed three hard-boiled eggs, shell and all. Every now and then she bit her father's ear just because she was so pleased to see him. Mr Nelson, who had been asleep, suddenly came leaping over, and he rubbed his eyes in surprise when he caught sight of Captain Longstocking.

'Oh, so you've still got Mr Nelson,' said Captain Longstocking.

'Yes, rather, and I've other domestic animals, you know,' said Pippi, fetching the horse, and he, too, got a hard-boiled egg to chew.

Captain Longstocking was very pleased that his daughter had arranged things so cosily for herself at Villekulla Cottage, and he was glad that she had her suitcase of gold coins, so that she had not suffered want while he was away.

When everyone had had enough to eat, Captain Longstocking took a tom-tom out of his suitcase, one of those that the cannibals used to beat time on when they had their dancing and religious feasts. Captain Longstocking sat down on the floor and beat the drum. It sounded muffled and eerie, different from anything that Tommy and Annika had ever heard.

'It's cannibalish,' said Tommy by way of explanation to Annika.

Pippi took her big shoes off and danced in her stockinged feet a dance which was eerie, too. Finally King Ephraim danced a savage war dance which he had learnt at Canny-Canny Island. He swung a spear and gesticulated wildly with the shield and stamped so hard with his bare feet that Pippi shouted:

'Watch out, or the kitchen floor will crack!'

'Won't matter,' said Captain Longstocking,

whirling on, 'cos now you're going to be a Cannibal Princess, daughter mine!'

Pippi darted forward and danced with her father. They posed to each other and heigh-hoed and shouted, sometimes taking such big leaps that Tommy and Annika felt dizzy from watching them. It seemed that Mr Nelson did, too, because he covered his eyes all the time.

Gradually the dancing changed into a wrestling match between Pippi and her father. Captain Longstocking threw his daughter so that she landed on the hat shelf. But she did not stay there long. With a yell she took a huge leap right across the kitchen straight for her father. A second later she had thrown him like a rocket head first into the wood-box. His fat legs were pointing straight up in the air. He could not get out by himself, partly because he was too fat and partly because he laughed so much. It sounded like the roar of thunder down in the wood-box. Pippi took hold of his feet to pull him up, but that made him laugh so much that he nearly choked. The fact was that he was extremely ticklish.

'D- d- d- don't t- t- t- ti- i- ck- ck- l- le me,' he groaned. 'You can throw me into the lake or heave me out of the window, anything, but d-d-d-don't t-t-t-ti-i-ck-ck-l-le me under my feet!'

He laughed so much that Tommy and Annika were afraid the wood-box might crack. At last he managed to wriggle out of the box. As soon as he was on his feet again, he made for Pippi and threw her right across the kitchen. She landed with her face on the stove which was full of soot.

'Ha-ha, here we have the Cannibal Princess— hey presto,' shouted Pippi with glee, turning a face as black as soot to Tommy and Annika. With a howl she threw herself on her father, giving him such a beating that his straw skirt crackled and clouds of straw whirled about the kitchen. The gold crown fell off and rolled under the table. In the end Pippi succeeded in throwing her father on to the floor and she sat down on him, saying:

'Do you give in?'

'I do,' said Captain Longstocking, and they both laughed so much that they cried and Pippi bit her father's nose lightly.

'I haven't enjoyed myself so much since you and I cleaned up that sailors' pub in Singapore!' he said.

He crawled under the table and picked up his crown.

'The cannibals should see this,' he said, 'the State Regalia lying under the kitchen table at Villekulla Cottage!'

He put on his crown and combed out the straw skirt which was looking rather thin.

'It seems to me that you'll have to send it for invisible mending,' said Pippi.

'It was worth it, though,' said Captain Longstocking.

He sat down on the floor and wiped the sweat from his brow.

'Well, Pippi, my child,' he said, 'd'you tell fibs at all nowadays?'

'Yes, I do, when I've got time, but that's not very often, I'm afraid,' said Pippi. 'And what about you? You weren't so bad at it either.'

'Oh, I usually tell the cannibals a few tall stories on Saturday nights if they've behaved well during the week. We generally have a little yarn and sing-song evening to the accompaniment of drums and torchlight dancing. The taller my stories the harder they beat the drums.'

'I see,' said Pippi, 'but no one beats the drum for me. Here I am all alone telling myself fibs that I'm simply full of and that it's a joy to hear, but no one even plays on a comb because of that. The other night when I'd gone to bed I thought up a long story about a calf who could make lace and climb trees—just imagine! I believed every word of it. But beat a drum! No, indeed! No one does that!'

'Well, then! *I'm* going to do it,' said Captain Longstocking. And he rolled the drum for a long time for his daughter, and Pippi sat on his lap with her sooty face against his cheek, so that he got as black as she was.

A thought had occurred to Annika. She did not know if it was proper for her to mention it, but she could not help doing so.

'It's wrong to tell lies,' she said. 'Mummy says so.'

'Don't be silly, Annika,' said Tommy. 'Pippi doesn't tell real lies, it's pretend lies. She makes up stories, you see.'

Pippi looked at Tommy thoughtfully.

'Sometimes you talk so wisely it makes me think you might be a great man one day,' she said.

Evening had come. It was time for Tommy and Annika to go home. It had been an eventful day and it was interesting to have seen a real live Cannibal King, and of course it was lovely for Pippi to have her father at home, but still . . . still . . .

When Tommy and Annika had crept into bed they did not talk as they usually did. There was complete silence in the nursery. Then a sigh was heard. It came from Tommy. After a time there was another sigh. This time it came from Annika.

'Why do you keep on sighing?' said Tommy irritably.

There was no reply. For Annika was underneath the bedclothes, weeping.

8
Pippi gives a Farewell Party

When Tommy and Annika walked
through the kitchen door of Villekulla
Cottage next morning, the whole house
was echoing with the most terrific snores. Captain
Longstocking had not yet woken up. Pippi,
however, was standing in the kitchen doing her
early morning exercises when Tommy and Annika
came and interrupted her.

'It's settled,' said Pippi. 'Now my future is
assured. I'm going to be a Cannibal Princess. For
six months in the year I'm going to be a Cannibal

Princess and for the other six I'm going to sail on all the oceans in the world in the *Hoppetossa*. Daddy thinks that if he rules firmly over the cannibals for six months in the year, they'll manage without a king for the other six months. You do see, don't you, that an old sea dog must feel a deck under his feet now and then? Besides, he must think of my education. If I'm to be a really good pirate one day, it won't do for me only to live at Court. It makes you soft, Daddy says.'

'Aren't you going to be at Villekulla Cottage at all?' asked Tommy in a small voice.

'Yes, when we retire,' said Pippi, 'in about fifty or sixty years' time. Then you and I can play and have a nice time together, can't we?'

Neither Tommy nor Annika could find much comfort in what she said.

'Imagine! A Cannibal Princess!' said Pippi dreamily. 'Not many children become that. I shall look grand! I shall have rings in all my ears and a slightly bigger ring in my nose.'

'What else are you going to wear?' asked Annika.

'Nothing else,' said Pippi. 'Not another scrap! But I shall have a cannibal of my own to polish me all over with shoe polish every morning. All I'll have to do will be to put myself in the passage at night together with my shoes.'

Tommy and Annika tried to picture what Pippi would look like.

'D'you think the black will look well with your red hair?' asked Annika doubtfully.

'We'll see,' said Pippi. 'If not, it's easy to dye hair green.' She sighed in rapture. 'Princess Pippilotta! What pomp! What grandeur! And how I shall dance! Princess Pippilotta dancing in the light of the camp fire to the rolling of drums. My goodness, how my nose ring will rattle then!'

'When—when—are you going?' asked Tommy. His voice sounded a little husky.

'The *Hoppetossa* is weighing anchor tomorrow,' said Pippi. All three children were silent for a long time. It seemed there was nothing more to be said. But at last Pippi turned a cartwheel and said:

'Tonight a farewell party will be held at Villekulla Cottage. A farewell party—I will say no more! Everyone who wants to come and say goodbye to me is welcome.'

The news spread like wild-fire among all the children of the little town.

'Pippi Longstocking is leaving town, and she is giving a farewell party tonight at Villekulla Cottage. Anybody who wants to can come!'

There were many who wanted to come; thirty-four children to be exact. Tommy and Annika had persuaded their mother to allow them to stay up as long as they liked that evening. Their mother realized that she could not do otherwise.

Tommy and Annika would never forget the evening when Pippi had her farewell party. It was one of those delightfully warm and beautiful summer evenings when you keep thinking: 'This is what it's really like when it's summer!'

All the roses in Pippi's garden glowed with colour and gave out their scent in the dusk. The old trees seemed to whisper secretly among themselves. It would all have been wonderful, if only—if only . . . Tommy and Annika did not want to think of the rest.

All the children from the town had brought their ocarinas. They blew them gaily as they came tramping up the garden path of Villekulla Cottage, led by Tommy and Annika. The moment they reached the steps to the porch the front door was thrown open and Pippi stood in the doorway. Her eyes shone in her freckled face.

'Welcome to my humble dwelling!' she said with a sweet smile. Annika took a long look at her so that she would always be able to remember what Pippi looked like. Never, never would she forget her, standing there with the red plaits and the freckles and the happy smile and the big black shoes.

Nearby there was the muffled beat of a drum. Captain Longstocking was sitting in the kitchen with the cannibal drum between his knees. He had dressed in his Cannibal King clothes today as well. Pippi had specially asked him to do so, because she knew that all the children would very much want to see a real live Cannibal King.

The whole kitchen became filled with children who crowded round King Ephraim to look at him. Annika thought it was lucky no more had come, because then there might not have been room for them. As she was thinking this the music from a concertina was heard in the garden. The entire crew of the *Hoppetossa* was coming, with Fridolf in the lead. It was Fridolf who was playing the concertina. Pippi had gone down to the harbour that same day to greet her friends and invite them to the farewell party. Now she rushed up to Fridolf and hugged him till his face began to go blue. Then she let him go, shouting:

'Music! Music!'

Then Fridolf played his concertina, King Ephraim beat his drum, and all the children blew their ocarinas.

The lid of the wood-box was shut and on it stood long rows of bottles of ginger beer. There were fifteen iced cakes on the big kitchen table, and a giant saucepan full of sausages on the stove.

King Ephraim began by grabbing eight sausages. Everyone followed his example, and soon the only sounds to be heard in the kitchen were those of sausages being munched. Then everyone was allowed to help himself to as much cake and ginger beer as he wanted. It was rather a squash in the kitchen, and the guests overflowed on to the porch and into the garden, and you could see the gleam of white icing here and there in the dusk.

When no one could possibly eat another thing Tommy suggested shaking down the sausages and the iced cakes with a game like 'Follow my leader', perhaps. Pippi did not know how to play it, so Tommy explained to her that someone had to be leader and all the others were to copy everything that the leader did.

'Right-o,' said Pippi. 'Doesn't sound a bad idea. I think I'd better be the leader.'

She began by climbing the shed roof. To get there she had first to climb the garden fence, and then she was able to edge herself up on her tummy on to the roof. Pippi and Tommy and Annika had done it so many times before that to them it was easy, but the other children thought it rather difficult. The sailors from the *Hoppetossa* were, of course, used to climbing the rigging so it was nothing to them, either, but Captain Longstocking got into difficulties because he was so fat, and also he got tangled up with his straw skirt. He breathed heavily as he heaved himself on to the roof.

'This straw skirt will never be the same again,' he said gloomily.

From the shed roof Pippi jumped down to the ground. Some of the younger children were, of course, afraid to do this, but Fridolf was a good sort. He lifted down all those who dared not jump. After that Pippi turned six somersaults on the lawn. They all copied her, but Captain Longstocking said:

'Someone will have to give me a push from behind, otherwise I shall never do it.'

Pippi did. She gave him such a big push that once he had started he could not stop, but rolled like a ball across the lawn and turned fourteen somersaults instead of six.

Then Pippi ran into Villekulla Cottage, racing up the porch steps, and climbed out through a window. By standing with her legs wide apart she could just reach a ladder outside. Quickly she skipped up the ladder, leapt on to the roof of Villekulla Cottage, rushed along the top of the roof, jumped up on the chimney and stood on one leg crowing like a cock. Then she threw herself head first into a tree by the side of the house, slid down to the ground, rushed into the wood-shed, caught hold of an axe and chopped down a plank in the wall, crept through the narrow chink, jumped up on the garden fence, walked along the top of the fence for fifty yards, climbed an oak and sat down to rest in the very top of it.

Quite a crowd of people had collected in the road outside Villekulla Cottage, and later they went home and told everybody that they had seen a Cannibal King standing on one leg on Villekulla Cottage's chimney shouting 'cock-a-doodle-do' so that you could hear it for miles. But no one believed them.

When Captain Longstocking tried to squeeze through the narrow hole in the wall of the wood-shed the inevitable happened—he got stuck and could move neither forwards nor backwards. That was why the game stopped short, and all the children gathered round to watch Fridolf sawing Captain Longstocking out of the wall.

'It was a rollicking good game,' said Captain Longstocking, very pleased when he was free again. 'What shall we think up next?'

'Years ago,' said Fridolf, 'the Cap'n and Pippi

used to have a match to see who was the strongest. It was good fun to watch.'

'Not a bad idea,' said Captain Longstocking, 'but the worst of it is that my daughter is getting to be stronger than me.'

Tommy was standing close to Pippi.

'Pippi,' he whispered, 'I was so 'fraid that you were going to creep into our hiding-place in the oak when we played "Follow my leader". I don't want anyone else to know about it. Not even if we never go there again.'

'No, it's our secret,' said Pippi.

Her father took hold of an iron poker. He bent it in the middle as if it had been made of wax. Pippi took another poker and did the same.

'That's nothing,' she said, 'I used to amuse myself with simple tricks like that when I was in my cradle. Just to pass the time.'

At this Captain Longstocking unhinged the kitchen door. Fridolf and five other sailors stood on the door and Captain Longstocking lifted them all high in the air and carried them round the lawn ten times.

It was now quite dark, so Pippi fixed burning torches here and there and they shone beautifully, casting a fairy light over the garden.

'Are you ready now?' she said to her father after the tenth round. He was. So Pippi put the horse on the kitchen door and on the horse's back she put Fridolf and three of the other sailors, and each of the four had two children in their arms. Fridolf held Tommy and Annika. Then Pippi lifted the kitchen door and carried them round the lawn twenty-five times. It looked marvellous in the light from the torches.

' 'Pon my word, child, you *are* stronger than me,' said Captain Longstocking.

After that everyone sat down on the lawn and Fridolf played the concertina, and all the other sailors sang the most beautiful sea shanties. The children danced to the music. Pippi took a torch in each hand and danced more wildly than anyone.

The party ended with a firework display. Pippi set off rockets and Catherine wheels, so that the whole sky hissed with them. Annika sat in the porch watching. It was all so very beautiful. So truly lovely. She could not now see the roses, but she could smell them in the darkness. How wonderful it would all have been if only—if only . . . An icy hand seemed to clutch at Annika's heart. Tomorrow—what would things be like then? And all the rest of the summer holidays? And forever? There would be no Pippi at Villekulla Cottage any more. There would be no Mr Nelson, and no horse standing in the porch. No more rides, no outings with Pippi, no pleasant evening hours in the kitchen of Villekulla Cottage, no tree where ginger beer grew. Well, the tree would be there, of course, but Annika had a strong feeling that there would not be any ginger beer growing in it when Pippi was gone. What would she and Tommy do tomorrow? Play croquet, probably. Annika sighed.

The party was over. All the children said thank you and goodbye. Captain Longstocking went back with his sailors to the *Hoppetossa*. He thought Pippi might as well come, too. But Pippi said she wanted to stay one more night at Villekulla Cottage.

'Tomorrow morning at ten o'clock we weigh anchor, don't forget,' shouted Captain Longstocking as he went.

Now only Pippi and Tommy and Annika were left. They sat silent on the porch steps in the darkness.

'Do come here and play just the same,' said Pippi at last. 'The key will be hanging on a nail beside the door. You can have everything in the drawers. And if I put a ladder inside the oak, you can climb down there by yourselves, although there might not be quite so much ginger beer growing. It's the wrong time of year.'

'No, Pippi,' said Tommy solemnly, 'we shall never come here again.'

'No! Never, never,' said Annika, thinking that after this she would shut her eyes every time she had to pass Villekulla Cottage. Villekulla Cottage without Pippi . . .

9

Pippi goes Aboard

Pippi carefully locked the door of Villekulla Cottage. She hung the key on a nail just beside it. She lifted the horse from the porch—lifted him from the porch for the very last time. Mr Nelson was already sitting on her shoulder looking important. He seemed to realize that something unusual was about to happen.

'Well, I suppose that's all,' said Pippi.

Tommy and Annika nodded. Yes, they supposed it was.

'We're quite early,' said Pippi. 'Let's walk and then it'll take longer.'

Tommy and Annika nodded again, but said nothing. They began their walk to the town. To the harbour. To the *Hoppetossa*. They left the horse to follow as he pleased.

Pippi glanced back over her shoulder at Villekulla Cottage.

'Not a bad cottage that,' she said. 'Free from fleas and pleasant in every way. I may not be able to say that much for the cannibal mud hut where I'm going to live from now on.'

Tommy and Annika said nothing.

'If there should be a terrible lot of fleas in my cannibal mud hut,' continued Pippi, 'I shall tame them and keep them in a cigar box and play with them in the evenings. I shall tie little bows round their legs and the two most faithful and most affectionate fleas I shall call "Tommy" and "Annika" and they're going to sleep in my bed at night.'

Not even this roused Tommy and Annika from their silence.

'What on earth's the matter with you two?' said Pippi irritably. 'I can tell you it's jolly dangerous to be silent for long. Your tongue shrivels up if you don't use it. I once knew a fireplace builder in Calcutta who kept on being

116

silent. Perhaps you can imagine what happened. Once he wanted to say to me, "Goodbye, dear Pippi, happy voyage and thanks for everything!" And can you guess what became of it? First he screwed his face up dreadfully, because the hinges of his mouth had gone completely rusty, so I had to oil them with sewing-machine oil, then out came, "Coo pi ank ing!" I then took a look in his mouth, and would you believe it? There lay his tongue like a withered little leaf! And as long as he lived that fireplace builder could never say anything except "Goo pi ank ing!" It would be dreadful if the same thing happened to you. Let's see if you can say it better than the fireplace builder: "Happy voyage, dear Pippi, and thanks for everything!" Try!'

'Happy voyage, dear Pippi, and thanks for everything,' said Tommy and Annika obediently.

'Thank goodness for that,' said Pippi. 'You certainly gave me a fright! If you'd said, "Coo pi ank ing" I don't know what I should have done.'

There was the harbour. There lay the *Hoppetossa*. Captain Longstocking stood on deck, shouting his orders. The sailors rushed to and fro to make everything ready for departure. On the quay all the people in the little town had gathered to wave goodbye to Pippi, and there she was together with Tommy and Annika and the horse and Mr Nelson.

'Here's Pippi Longstocking! Make way for Pippi Longstocking!' the folk cried, and stood aside to let Pippi pass. Pippi waved and greeted people to right and left. Then she took the horse and carried him up the gangway. The poor animal glowered suspiciously round him, for horses do not like boat trips much.

'So there you are, dear child,' said Captain Longstocking, breaking off in the middle of an order to give Pippi a hug. They squeezed each other till their ribs creaked.

Annika had been going around with a lump in her throat all morning, and when she saw Pippi lifting the horse on board the lump loosened. Standing pressed against a packing-case on the quay she began to cry, at first quietly, but gradually more and more loudly.

'Shut up,' said Tommy angrily. 'You're disgracing us in front of everybody!'

This only resulted in Annika bursting into an absolute flood of tears. She wept so much that she quivered. Tommy gave a stone such a kick that it rolled down over the edge of the quay and fell into the water. Actually he would have liked to have thrown it at the *Hoppetossa*. Miserable boat to take Pippi from them! In fact, if no one had been looking, Tommy would have liked to cry a little too. But that would not do. He kicked another stone savagely.

Now Pippi came running down the gangway from the ship. She made straight for Tommy and Annika. She clasped their hands in hers.

'Ten minutes left,' she said.

Then Annika threw herself down across a packing-case and wept as if her heart would break. There were no more stones for Tommy to kick. He clenched his teeth and looked very, very angry.

All the children in the town crowded round Pippi. They brought out their ocarinas and played a farewell tune for her. It sounded dreadfully sad, because it was a very, very plaintive tune. Annika was now weeping so much that she could hardly stand upright. At that moment Tommy remembered that he had written a little farewell rhyme in Pippi's honour. He hauled out a paper and began to read. Only it was awful that his voice should tremble so!

'Farewell, Pippi dear, you leave us now,
But remember how
Good friends you've here always
For all your days.'

'Gosh, it rhymed!' said Pippi, pleased. 'I shall

learn it by heart and say it to the cannibals when we're sitting round the camp fire at night.'

The children were pressing in from every direction to say goodbye. Pippi raised her hand to call for silence.

'Children,' she said, 'after this I shall only have little cannibal children to play with. What we're going to amuse ourselves with I don't know. Perhaps we'll play catch with rhinoceroses, and do snake charming, and ride on elephants and put up a swing in the coconut palm round the corner. I expect we'll manage to pass the time somehow.'

Pippi paused. Both Tommy and Annika felt they hated those cannibal children that Pippi was going to play with from now on.

'But,' continued Pippi, 'there may come a day during the rainy season—a boring day, because even if it's fun to skip about without clothes on when it's raining, you can't do more than get really wet; and when we've done that properly perhaps we'll crawl into my mud hut, provided it hasn't all turned into clay, of course, because in that case we can make mud pies, but if it hasn't turned into clay we'll sit down inside, the cannibal children and I, and then perhaps the cannibal children will say, "Pippi, tell us a story"! Then I shall tell about a tiny little town which is far far away in another part of the world, and about the little white children who live there. "You can't imagine what dear children they are," I shall tell the cannibal children. "They're white like little angels all over except their feet, they play ocarinas, and—best of all—they know pluttification." Only the little black cannibal children might get upset that *they* don't know pluttification, and then I shan't know what to do with them. Well, if the worst comes to the worst, I'll have to pull down the mud hut and make clay of it and then we can make mud pies and dig ourselves down into the clay right up to our necks. By that time I should be much surprised if I hadn't managed to make them think of something else besides pluttification. Thank you, all of you! And goodbye very much!'

The children blew on their ocarinas an even sadder tune than before.

'Pippi, it's time to go on board,' called Captain Longstocking.

'Aye, aye, Cap'n,' said Pippi.

She turned to Tommy and Annika, gazing at them.

Her eyes look queer, thought Tommy. His mother had looked just like that once when Tommy was very, very ill. Annika was lying in a little heap on the packing-case. Pippi lifted her up in her arms.

'Goodbye, Annika, goodbye,' she whispered. 'Don't cry!'

Annika threw her arms round Pippi's neck and made a mournful sound.

'Goodbye, Pippi,' she managed to sob.

Then Pippi took Tommy's hand and squeezed it hard. She ran up the gangway. That was when a big tear rolled down Tommy's nose. He clenched his teeth, but it was no use. Another tear came. He took hold of Annika's hand, and together they stood there watching Pippi. They could see her up on deck, but things are always rather blurred when you see them through a mist of tears.

'Three cheers for Pippi Longstocking,' shouted the people on the quay.

'Pull up the gangway, Fridolf,' shouted Captain Longstocking.

Fridolf did so. The *Hoppetossa* was ready for her voyage to foreign parts. But then—

'Daddy,' shouted Pippi. 'I can't! I can't bear it!'

'What is it you can't bear?' asked Captain Longstocking.

'I can't bear that anyone on God's green earth should weep and be sad because of me, least of all

Tommy and Annika. Put the gangway down again! I'm staying at Villekulla Cottage.'

Captain Longstocking said nothing for some minutes.

'You do as you think best,' he said at last. 'You always did!'

Pippi nodded in agreement.

'Yes, I always did,' she said quietly.

Pippi and her father hugged each other again so that their ribs creaked, and they agreed that Captain Longstocking would come and see Pippi at Villekulla Cottage very often.

'When it comes to the point, Daddy,' said Pippi, 'it's really best for a child to have a proper home and not wander about on the sea so much and live in cannibal huts, don't you think?'

'You're right as always, my daughter,' said Captain Longstocking. ''Course your life is more regular at Villekulla Cottage, and I'm sure that's best for little children.'

'Exactly,' said Pippi, 'it's definitely best for little children to have a regular life, especially if they can regulate it themselves.'

And so Pippi said goodbye to the sailors on the *Hoppetossa* and hugged her father a last time. Then she lifted the horse in her strong arms and carried him down the gangway. The anchor of the

Hoppetossa was hauled up. At the last moment an idea occurred to Captain Longstocking.

'Pippi,' he shouted, 'you must have some more gold coins! Catch!'

And he threw across another case of gold coins, but unfortunately the *Hoppetossa* was too far away and the case missed the quay. There was a splash and the case sank. There was a murmur of disappointment among the crowd of people. Then there was another splash. That was Pippi diving. In a moment she rose clutching the case between her teeth. She climbed up on the quay, at the same time pulling away some seaweed which was clinging behind her ear.

'Ha, I'm rich as a troll again,' she said.

Tommy and Annika had not yet grasped what was happening. They were staring open-mouthed at Pippi and the horse and Mr Nelson and the case and the *Hoppetossa* which was steering with full sail out of the harbour.

'Aren't you—aren't you going in the ship?' said Tommy doubtfully at last.

'Guess three times,' said Pippi, wringing the water out of her plaits.

Then she lifted Tommy and Annika and the suitcase and Mr Nelson up on the horse and swung herself up behind them.

'Back to Villekulla Cottage,' she shouted loudly.

Then at last it was all clear to Tommy and Annika. Tommy was so thrilled that he instantly started on his favourite song:

'Here come the Swedes with a hullabaloo!'

Annika had cried so much that she could not stop immediately. She was still sobbing, but they were happy little sobs which would soon cease. Pippi's arms were firmly round her. It felt wonderfully safe. Oh, how wonderful everything was!

'What shall we do, today, Pippi?' asked Annika when she had stopped sobbing.

'Well—play croquet, perhaps,' said Pippi.

'Let's,' said Annika. She knew that even croquet would be quite different with Pippi.

'Or else,' said Pippi thinking.

All the children in the little town crowded round the horse to hear what Pippi was saying.

'Or else,' she said. 'Or else we might nip down to the stream and practise walking on the water.'

'You can't walk on the water,' said Tommy.

'Oh yes, it's not at all impossible,' said Pippi. 'In Cuba I once met a carpenter who . . . '

The horse started galloping and the little children who were crowding round could not hear the rest. But for a long, long time they stood looking after Pippi and her horse galloping in the direction of Villekulla Cottage. Soon all they could see was a small dot far away. Finally it disappeared altogether.

About the author

Astrid Lindgren was born in Vimmerby, Sweden in 1907. She married Sture Lindgren in 1931 and had a son and a daughter. Pippi Longstocking was created when Astrid made up a story about an extremely strong, red-haired girl for her daughter who was ill with pneumonia.

The first Pippi Longstocking book was published in Sweden in 1945 and was an instant hit with children, although some adults feared that Pippi was a bit too independent and perhaps unsuitable for girls to read. In the end though everyone agreed that Pippi was a wonderful and endearing character and her stories have since been published all over the world, including the English translation published in 1954.

Astrid Lindgren wrote over 40 books for children and broadcast widely on TV and radio—reading her stories.

In 1989 a theme park dedicated to the author—Astrid Lindgren Varld—was opened in her home town of Vimmerby.

Astrid Lindgren was the recipient of many major awards for her writing, including the prestigious Hans Christian Andersen Award and The International Book Award. She died in 2002 at the age of 94.

Other books by Astrid Lindgren

Pippi is nine years old. She lives alone in her own
house with a horse and a monkey, and she does
exactly as she pleases. She has no mother and she believes
her father is the king of a cannibal island. She has never
learnt to look after herself and has never been to school.
Her friends, Tommy and Annika, are green with envy—but
although they have to go to school and go to bed
when they are told, they still have time to join
Pippi on all her great adventures.

ISBN 978-0-19-275413-4

Pippi Longstocking and her friends, Tommy and
Annika, set off on their greatest adventure of all—a
trip to Canny Canny Island, the home of Pippi's
cannibal king father. They explore caves, play marbles
with real pearls, and the pirates and sharks they meet
prove no match for Pippi! But will they all be
home in time for Christmas?

ISBN 978-0-19-275481-3

Other Oxford Fiction

How to Survive Summer Camp

Jacqueline Wilson

ISBN 978-0-19-272704-6

Typical! Mum and Uncle Bill have gone off on a swanky honeymoon, while Stella's been dumped at Evergreen Summer Camp. Guess what? She's not happy about it!

Things get worse. Stella loses all her hair (by accident!), has to share a dorm with snobby Karen and Louise, and is forced into terrifying swimming lessons with Uncle Pong! It looks as if she's in for a nightmare summer—how can Stella possibly survive?

A hilarious summer story from the award-winning author of *Double Act, Bad Girls,* and *The Suitcase Kid.*

The Tales of Olga da Polga
Michael Bond
ISBN 978-0-19-275495-0

Olga da Polga is no ordinary guinea-pig. She's a very special guinea-pig indeed ... and she knows it!

From the minute Olga arrives at her new home, she gathers all the other animals in the garden around and starts telling them exciting tales about all the wild and wonderful adventures she's had. Sometimes the other animals aren't sure whether to believe her or not—but surely Olga wouldn't be making them up, would she?

Olga Meets Her Match
Michael Bond
ISBN 978-0-19-275494-3

The Sawdust family decide Olga needs a holiday, so off she goes for a break by the sea. During her stay she becomes friends with Boris, a Russian guinea-pig, and is surprised to discover that Boris has as many stories to tell as she does!

Smile!
Geraldine McCaughrean
ISBN 978-0-19-271961-4

When Flash crashes in the middle of a desert, he finds himself injured and alone, armed with nothing but a cheap instant camera. Then out of the sunlight appears a girl in a scarlet dress ...

Sutira and her little brother take Flash home. The people of her village have never met a photographer—never seen a photo—but photography is the kind of magic everyone has a use for.

Flash has only ten pictures left in his camera. How can he best use them to make his new friends smile?

'An uplifting, feel-good story.'   *Bookfest*

Winner of the Smarties Bronze Award